Yesterday

is Ours

By HJ Bellus

Yesterday is Ours

Limitless Publishing, LLC
Kailua, HI 96734
www.limitlesspublishing.com

Formatting: Limitless Publishing

ISBN-13: 978-1-64034-572-0
ISBN-10: 1-64034-572-8

Dedication

To my girls…Michelle, Diane, and Stacy Jo. You girls always have my back and believe in my words. You may never know how much I appreciate you. Thank you, and this one is for you with every shade of yellow and one very naughty dog.

Prologue

Cody

The flames from the bonfire lick and lap at the star-dabbled sky. Tailgates, wild dreams, and best friends are what fill my high school years. I'm the king on top of the world. A sweet smell of coconut tangled with lime assaults me. That simple scent intoxicates me. Always has since Roberta Cooper started wearing it during seventh grade.

Pretty damn sure I fell in love with the blonde-haired, blue-eyed beauty when the elementary principal introduced her to our second-grade class. She had tears spilling down her face when her pencil didn't fit in the standard pencil sharpener in our classroom. I was there by her side and have never left it. We've been through scraped knees, tetherball champions, the awkward middle school years, broken bones and signed casts with hearts and all, and now hopelessly in love our senior year.

Jessie and Jules cuddle together on the tailgate of

his truck. Their story is much the same. They don't fly under the radar. Instead, they are the icons of the town. Homecoming queen and star athlete—they run this place. Pretty sure every citizen of Boone would elect them the mayor of the town in a heartbeat even though they are high school seniors.

Brady and Tessi perch themselves on opposite sides of his tailgate. They play it off well. Tessi and Jules are inseparable, and Brady hangs with Jessie and me. Brady and Tessi have the game of hating each other down to a tee. If I was a betting man, and I am so this is gospel, the two of them will end up hitched with two-point-five kids in the future, picket fence and all.

My favorite smell hits me again, and I glance away from my friends and fire down to the wild soul snuggled next to me. Roberta Cooper, also known as Bertie. She'll always be my Bertie. My girl is a blonde-haired beauty and owns my soul. She's mine. There was never any doubt, and honestly, neither of us ever had a choice. The force of the world threw us together.

We are settled on a log with my girl curling from her cuddled position in my lap and wrapping herself around me. My truck is parked in the distance on purpose. I've always been a confident person up until this moment. It's our time. We've been official since our freshman year. Everyone in our county knows Bertie is mine. No one dares look her way a second longer than necessary.

My girl isn't the homecoming queen, cheerleader, or miss popular. Nope, she'll go down in the yearbooks as the nerdy girl who always had her nose stuck in a book, and that's what I love about her most. She has her grandma, who loves her dearly and raises her, her textbooks, and me.

Brady howls along with" "She's Got It All" by Kenny Chesney while the rest of the clan snickers and tips back red Solo cups. I find myself whispering the words of the song into Bertie's ear. This sweet little one has no idea how she has all my attention. When her hands drift to places that make me stutter over the words of the song, I struggle to remain where we are planted on the old drift log, perfectly placed by the bonfire. What is about to happen will be a memory in all my years I will never forget.

"I'm ready." A sweet whisper tickles against my neck.

I glance down at the blonde beauty in my arms, her ocean blue eyes dazzling at me. My arms squeeze tighter around her, wanting to remember it all. When the song changes, I stand up with her in my arms. I'll carry this woman wherever we go.

"Gonna head out," I announce to the group.

"Just Like Jesse James" by Cher starts playing, prompting Jessie and Jules to do their own version of Dirty Dancing on the tailgate. Not one of our best friends pays any attention to us. Bertie tucks her face into my neck, peppering sweet kisses along my skin, and that's all I need to move forward.

I know these backwoods better than anyone around. It's been my playground since I knew how to walk. My parents were more concerned about society and how much money was stuffed in their pockets. They had a child for the sake of having one since it was what society deemed appropriate. The laws of the universe weren't on their side when this smartass redneck hillbilly plopped in their lap.

"You know I can just kiss the hell out of you if you change your mind, right?" I kiss the top of her head, tightening my grip around her.

"I know, Cody." She reaches up, stroking her finger down my jaw. "But I'm so ready."

A gasp escapes Bertie when she sees the lit candles, fluffy-ass pillows, and red plaid flannel blankets. She had earlier shared with me that it was her ideal setting for our first time. I didn't let her down, even though it took me driving three hours to get the right bedding. Echoes of our friends belting out a favorite Garth Brooks song surrounds us.

"Should've parked further away." I set Bertie on the tailgate, nesting between her spread legs. I run my palms up and down her jean-clad thighs.

"I can only hear the sound of your heartbeat drumming along with the rhythm of mine." She cups my cheeks, dipping for a kiss. It's sweet, tender, and hot as hell.

I know I won't be able to stop myself tonight. I grab her by the hips, scooting her back and hopping in the back of the truck, covering her body while not breaking the kiss. Our clothing is tossed piece by piece until we are cocooned in the thick flannel blanket. Bertie is the brave one, kissing the hell out of me through each step until there's nothing but blank space. Once we are connected, there's nothing else left worth in this world.

She's mine.

Forever.

End of.

***

Years Later

Boone Leader

Lead Story

Local hero, Cody Sterling, stormed into a burning building. Late last night, one of our own volunteer firefighters saved the day by rushing into a fiery inferno to save a local kindergarten teacher, Kate Wilson-Valentukonis. Kate is new to our town but is already a beloved teacher by many five- and six-year-olds, and their parents, in our community. The horrific incident has broken many of our hearts. The evil actions of those responsible is something none of us can begin to process.

Cody and Kate have both been transported to the local hospital in critical condition. We know both flirted with death, but it was Cody's bravery that gave them hope.

The two suspects who started the fire were shot by police when they wouldn't give themselves up or put down their weapons.

Our small town has been rocked by this event. The one thing we can cling to is the good in the world. It's safe to say our little town is praying for a speedy recovery for both Cody Sterling and Kate Wilson-Valentukonis.

Chapter 1

Cody

The boys brought me here. The five-hour drive was bathed in silence. They tried to talk about nonsense and shit, yet all I had to give was a jerk of my chin. I'm a skeleton of a man, fighting every day to get out of the shadows. It's the pain that holds me back. They think it's the scars and marks on my skin. They couldn't be further from the truth. I've never corrected them.

Feeling fractured bones that have tried to mend creak and crack as you simply try to piss or take a shit isn't something any man would offer willingly. Truly thought I was at my lowest the day I ran off Bertie. Roberta Cooper, the one girl who owned me, and I ruined it all being cocky and drunk. I fucked her roommate. Lied to her and pushed her out of my life. Told Bertie that we were on different paths when really I was covering up a soul-deep secret that would ruin us. I never wanted her to feel that pain. A

6

chicken-shit move, and one I've had to live with.

I know how it feels because my body is so fucked up right now I don't know what normal feels like. I vowed that day she'd never know what I did, and I've kept good on that secret for years upon years.

"Let's taste the chocolate pudding before we go." Jessie shoves Max in the shoulder. "You know, since that's our boy's favorite."

"I was thinking of ordering a Pussy Pleaser." Max smirks.

"Just leave," I grumble, tamping down the growl that yearns to shred from my chest as I sit down on the edge of the bed.

They checked me in and are pushing the limits of waiting, long enough to make me uncomfortable. I guess that's what life-long friends do. The harder they try to bring me back to life, the further I tumble down the dark, murky hole of hell. My personal hell. My body doesn't work, my mind has spiraled into a vortex of everything I've done wrong, and I'm at a loss on how to live.

My bar used to be my baby, and now I couldn't give two fucks. Haven't returned a call or talked to my parents. They only reached out because me saving a woman in a burning building was headline news on all major news station outlets around us. I swear it's the only time they've ever showed me attention. I made them damn proud opening a bar and acting the fool for years...not. It's a damn simple equation. I hate life right now.

"Cody." Jessie settles into the chair next to the hospital bed. "We aren't leaving until we know you're good."

I snort and shake my head, feeling like a bigger asshole. They'll never understand that it wasn't the fire. Well, it was the fire that brought the façade of my life tumbling down around my boots. It's nobody's fault, and I will never regret racing into the fiery house. I'd do it over again any day, knowing damn well Max, Jessie, or Brady would do the same thing.

It's the healing scars and the pain radiating from my hips every time I move that remind me of all my past blunders. I've fucked up so many times and masked it all with my charming personality.

The thing is when you fake it for so long, you'll eventually crumble like a deck of cards until your core is exposed to the world. That's something that would bring the greatest superhero to their knees.

I keep my gaze focused on the tile of the hospital room. "Get on back, you two, to your women and family. I'm good."

There's silence that's awkward as fuck. I don't dare look up. Walls would close in on me since I know my best friends can see right through me.

Jessie is the first to clear his throat. I feel a pat on my shoulder. "You got this, Cody. Will be expecting a cold one at your bar in a few months."

Max follows, saying much of the same.

"You got it, brothers," I mumble.

There's no footsteps or slamming of the door to my room. Not even an obnoxious nurse races in.

Jessie clears his throat again, and that's when I glance up. His knitted brows devastate me. The grief tensed up in his shoulders makes me feel like the bastard I am. My fingers itch for the vodka bottle. I drank my own damn self out of my bar. I'd give anything to just have a drink to numb this pain.

"We are here. I know you're struggling. I get that shit more than anyone. Just know you have a family to turn to that won't judge you."

I nod, giving him nothing else. It means the fucking world since my own parents are worthless in my eyes. I was the rich kid in high school. Looking back, it was cool as hell, but now it's worthless. Mom and Dad are jet setting the world while I'm left here shattered beyond belief. It goes far beyond the scars on my skin. Nobody will ever understand. I've always been carefree and up for the party. The thing is those years have caught up with me, and now I sit on a hospital bed, a shell of a man.

"I'm good here." I scrub the stubble on my jaw, where I tend to keep it clean-shaven. "I'll update you once my hip surgery is done."

The improving wounds of the burns are just that, and damn near healed. My left calf is covered in burns, as is my back. I guess that's a blessing, so I don't have to face them every day.

I get around like a ninety-year-old man, feeling the raging pain with each movement. This surgery should've been done before I went home, but I refused, not wanting to face shit. This is the first step to getting my life back and facing my past, or at least that's what I keep telling myself.

A king who once had it all sits here a broken and shattered man. I have glimpses of strength and guess I acted on that shit. I'm ready for the pain to be gone, then I'll deal with the internal bullshit.

"Yeah." Jessie gives a jerk of his chin.

I know what he's worried about. No need to ask him to know he's wondering if I'll skip out before the surgery is actually done. Max and Jessie took me to a rehabilitation place, and I lasted a whole whopping nine days. They forced me, and I didn't want to be there. It all went to hell. I returned home an even grumpier son of a bitch. Learning how to live after the accident wasn't even close to being on my radar.

I kick my legs up on the hospital bed, relaxing back, propping my arms behind my head as if I was in some damn fancy resort. I let loose my signature wisecrack smile. The first part of this process is re-training my mind to think positive.

"I've been a dick and in a shit state of mind. Thank you, brothers, for remaining by my side. Go crack a case open for me at the bar and enjoy it while I'm gone. I'll be home before you know it, limp free and all." I wink.

"There's our brother." Max walks over and pats me on the shoulder.

"Damn right you will be." Jessie flanks my other side.

"Coming back stronger and better." The words taste bitter on my tongue, but I force them out anyway.

"I'll hold off the family as long as I can. Sure won't be long with Emma and Finn wanting to see their favorite uncle," Jessie adds.

"Get out of here." I swat at both of them. "Meet with the surgeon tonight and then it's on."

They don't have to say a word for me to tell they feel like shit leaving me here alone. I've told them over and over that shit doesn't bother me. Never has. I guess when you're raised that way, it's what you know. Doesn't mean there aren't moments in time when I sure wish one blonde bombshell was by my side throughout life. I shake that shit off before I'm consumed into a vortex of memories.

The boys eventually take off, and I don't have a moment of time to myself before the nurses and staff at the surgery center finish checking me in.

Chapter 2

Cody

The stiff sheets of the hospital bed are already scratching against my ass. It's going to be a long damn night, that's for sure. Not to mention the stale smell in this place and the constant buzzing noises. I've already fine-tuned myself to block out the pages announced on the overhead speaker. The blood pressure cuff going off what seems every few minutes on my bicep is another damn story.

"Knock, knock." A grey-haired man in a white coat rounds into my room. His attention is laser-focused on a tablet in one hand while he scrubs his cheek with the other. "Mr. Sterling, how are we this evening?"

I find it odd he still doesn't look up at me. Not even once. His bedside manners are lacking at best. I did my research and know he's the best around when it comes to a total hip replacement. I had other options, but this man is the best and most aggressive.

"Good," I answer with one word.

"Looks like everything is set for tomorrow. All your labs look great." He relaxes in a chair next to my bed. "Do you have any questions?"

I shake my head. "No."

He ignores my answer and proceeds to explain to me the fact I'll be up and walking and it will take three to six weeks of recovery. He clears his throat mid-sentence.

"And you'll need to follow through with some therapy."

I pick up on the way he draws out "some therapy." Yeah, pretty damn hard to explain that I need some mental health counseling to live with my past sins and my current situation.

"Looks like a total month's stay if you buckle down and get through everything." Doctor Rayson finally makes eye contact with me.

I nod, having nothing to say to him.

"Well, I'll see you bright and early. Make sure you get plenty of rest or as much as you can in this zoo." He grins as a monitor serenades us from somewhere out in the hall.

A young nurse bursts into the room. "Excuse me, Doctor Rayson. Doctor Cooper has been paging you. It's urgent."

He nods, slowly rising from his chair. I notice he winces as he does, rubbing his chest. It's evident the surgeon is exhausted. He's the best in the state, so I don't worry about the fatigue or his awkward presence.

He doesn't bother himself with a goodbye as he groans and rushes from the room. I'm left staring at the white walls of the room. The journal Jules gave me to write feelings or some shit in lies on my bedside table. The spine is still stiff and unbroken and will remain that way. I'm not about to burst the jar of crap open tonight.

The night flies by once two nurses come in and out of my room getting my IV in and recording my vitals. It's annoying as hell, even though one of the nurses is hot as hell. She has an ass that would make any man dumb. And the fact I'm an ass man doesn't help me in the least. She's generous as she leans across me to hook up tubes, allowing her plump tits to graze my chest.

Before the fire, something like this would get me hot and bothered, ready to tango in the sheets. Now, not even a stirring happens besides the fact I'm appraising what the good Lord gave her. It's another reminder I've got to get my head screwed back on.

The two nurses gave up on talking to me, so they engaged in a personal conversation.

"Did you see the size of the ring?" the older brunette asks while fiddling with a machine.

The bombshell nods with her eyes going all glowy like women do when diamonds come into the conversation. "It's gorgeous, but there's just something off about him. I can't put my finger on it."

"You've always said that. You're crazy, Britt, and the only one that thinks that."

"Well, if a man ever puts a ring on my finger like that one, he'd best have only eyes for me and his flirting gear turned to low." Her cheeks blush a bright red.

Shit, all I need is popcorn at this point.

"He's friendly. Nothing wrong with that." The older nurse winks.

I clear my throat, curious as hell at this point. "Is this some reality show you're talking about?"

God knows I need something to pass the time. If I'm lucky, this show will be on Hulu.

Both nurses turn to me as if they were busted with their hand in the cookie jar. The older one is the first to talk. She brushes her bangs back and shakes her head.

"Sorry, we shouldn't have been talking about that."

"So, it's not a reality show?" I crook up an eyebrow.

"No," Britt shakes her head, "co-workers. So not professional of us."

"You were so quiet," Amber responds, or at least that's what her name badge reads. "But it's no excuse."

I wave them both off, seeing the stress painted on their faces and dancing in their features. "No worries. Sounded hella entertaining, and a man in my position could use some of that right about now."

Amber lets out a bated breath and rushes from the room with no further explanation. Britt relaxes on the bottom of the bed.

"Well, since we've already gossiped way too much in front of a patient...It's about two doctors here. Everyone is all goo-goo gah-gah over the new surgeon, and well, I think he's a slimeball. I've seen and heard things, but I'm just here for a paycheck, you know?"

"I get that." I nod, finding it pleasant how easy it

is to talk to her. Even though she's hot and right up my alley, not one single thought drifts that way.

"Enough about that." She smiles at me. "How do you feel about tomorrow? Doctor Rayson is amazing."

"Nervous as hell." I slide up further in the bed. "You gonna make sure the saw blades are sharpened?"

Her eyes go wide, but when she realizes a smirk plays out on my face, she giggles. I've always been known for my carefree humor and light-going attitude. Feels damn good to get a glimpse of that back.

"I'll make sure you get the sharpest." She pats the bed as she stands up. "Just push the button if you need anything. I'm here all night."

"Will do."

Right before she's about to round the corner out of my room, I holler her name.

"Britt."

The crazy curls bundled high on top of her head whip back my direction.

"Got any suggestions for mindless television shows to pass the time?"

She taps the center of her chin a few times. "I love *Grey's Anatomy*, but not tonight for you because, well…"

"People kick the bucket because of shit care." I grin wide.

Her smile matches mine. "Yeah, probably not the best. How about *Survivor*?"

"I'll check it out." I wink, not telling her *Survivor* is my freaking jam and I've watched every single episode ever aired. Shit, my bar, Cody's Shaggin' Shack, has a quiet hour when it airs. The only time you can ever hear a pin drop.

"It's my favorite. Absolute crazy fan here. I've even thought about submitting an application when they audition for fans."

God, to see her full ass in a little piece on my big screen at the bar does get something rustling under the scratchy hospital sheets. Not to mention what her tits would look like bouncing on the waves.

"When I get this bionic hip, let's give it a shot."

"Deal." Her one word comes out a half question and partially an answer.

I seal it with gusto. "Deal. Britt, our alliance has already been formed."

She shakes her head and disappears. A surge of energy bolts through my veins at the sensation of being the old Cody. It's way more addicting and exhilarating than what vodka ever did for me. I'm not saying Britt is the one by far, but it's energizing to talk to someone who isn't geared up to have a pity party in my honor.

I find myself grabbing the journal and pen attached to it. I smirk at the colossal flower hot glued to the top of it, knowing damn well it was one of Emma's craft projects. My family may not be blood, but it's way more powerful than any blood connection could ever hold. Jessie, Jules, and their three kids, Whit, Jack, and Emma. Then there's Max, who Jessie and Jules adopted. Hell, the kid became like mine when he moved back home.

I flip open the journal, coming face to face with a blank page. I find myself jotting down some of my favorite songs, ones that take me back to a time for when I'd give anything to have a redemption button. Johnny Cash, Fleetwood Mac, and several other artists begin to fill the blank space that used to haunt me. But now I find myself smiling at the memories dancing in my mind. It's all I have.

Chapter 3

Cody

Sleep was shit. Well, that's a lie. After I spilled out several song titles on the pages, I slept like a baby for a few hours. Better than I have been getting lately, but then it was the scratch and noise of the hospital keeping me up. I swear my eyelids would grow heavy and I'd be on my way slipping off into sleep, then bam, wide awake.

"It's the big day." Britt rounds into the room, tapping on an iPad.

"Awesome. Did you check that saw blade?" I grunt, pushing up in the bed.

"Yep, sharp as it comes." She winks at me.

This woman is a breath of fresh air. I can't quite place it, but it's comfortable with her. Britt's fine ass is just a cherry on top of the sundae.

"You pull an all-nighter?" I ask, doing my best to cover my morning wood. The thin hospital sheet is tenting into a towering teepee.

"Sure did. Getting you off into good hands and then I have a date with my pillow." She checks the monitors.

"You know you could bust me out of here and we could party together." My chest puffs up, feeling a bit of my old self flare to life. I'd never take her up on the offer if there was one. I mean, the old me was a gentleman taking the lady to dinner and offering her unlimited drinks.

"You're too much." She shakes her head.

A new nurse rushes into the room. I have no clue who she is, but I do know she is frazzled and upset. She shakes her head at Britt, and in the same moment, Britt's bright smile dims. I don't have to be a rocket scientist or even a damn surgeon to know something isn't right.

"What's going on?" I sit up taller in the bed, swinging my legs over the side of it, being careful of the tubes coming from my arms. My morning wood is a long ago thought.

"Nothing." Britt shakes her head and clears her throat. "A surgeon will be in soon to talk to you."

Panic strikes. Doctor Rayson said my bloodwork came back fine. Did they find something wrong, and now a doctor specializing in cancer or some other life-threatening disease is about to march their ass in here and break it to me?

The nurse of death or whatever you want to call her marches out of the room. My breathing quickens, and I'm ready to shred this room until I get some answers.

"Cody." Britt rests on the edge of my bed near my pillows, placing her hand on the top of my thigh.

"Nothing concerning you is wrong. I can't tell you anything else. It's nothing for you to panic over."

I clear my throat, trying not to sound panicked and freaked the hell out as I place my hand on top of hers and glance toward the door, waiting on the bad news to enter. "What in the fuck is going on?"

I don't even give two shits about the language I just dropped. Something is wrong and about to turn my world upside down. Britt is a kind and sexy-as-fuck nurse, and a gentle friend as I enter her world. It's evident in her adoring cocoa eyes as she continues to prove her soft touch and warmth on my skin. It's not the attraction hitting me strong for this woman; it's the missing puzzle piece of my life. I've missed the human touch. Just a simple hand-hold to let me know everything is going to be all right.

She's a great friend, even though it's been less than twelve hours. Britt has no idea who I am, what I own, or what I've done. It's unlike the prying stares in my hometown where everyone and their dog knows just how much money Cody has and whispers about the silver spoon stuck between my lips. I've never bothered to correct any of them. I didn't use a dime of my parents' money to build my business.

I shake the vortex of stupid shit from my mind. I'm a damn mess; there's no denying that. I open my mouth to speak.

"Britt," I grit out again. "I'm about to lose my shit. You evidently think I'm stronger than I am."

Her tender fingers graze the silver hair gracing my temples. Her plump lips part but nothing comes out. I'm dying to know what is dancing on her lips but continue to relish the joy of pure friendship.

"Excuse me." We whip both of our heads toward the sound of a foot stomp at the door of my room. "Whenever you two are ready, I'd like to meet with my patient."

Britt stiffens, straightening out her coarse teal scrubs and staring at a monitor near the corner of my bed. I want to pay attention to my new friend who seems desperate right now. But it's the blonde-haired raven clutching the iPad in her hands who catches my eye. It's the same woman who once owned my heart, and I tossed that love away.

Life has been damn good to her. She's no longer the string bean nerd I used to grow drunk on in high school. No, she's filled out so much more in the best possible ways. But there's no mistaking the worn and tired lines under her eyes.

"Sorry, Doctor Cooper, Cody was upset about not being taken into the operating room at his scheduled time. I'm—uh, trying to comfort him."

"Yeah." Bertie clicks her iPad alive. "Real grand of you, Britt."

Basically, short and to the point, the tension in the room is suffocating as hell. I find myself blinking once then twice before realizing the woman before me isn't a mirage. It's really her. The one soul I ever loved. It didn't end when I screwed up shit. Hell, no; I'd never be able to forget her. No amount of booze would ever diminish the flames of love I hold for her.

Britt dashes from the room without another word. I wince at the cruelty that just brushed through the room. Britt is an innocent party in this situation. I open my mouth then snap it shut. I have no damn idea what to say.

"Hey, how are you doing?" doesn't seem appropriate. I run my hands through my shaggy hair, knowing nothing I say will be worth it. I have no idea what to do or even how to feel. All I can seem to do is stare at her. This can't be my life.

And on the other hand, my head bounds and bounces off the walls of the suffocating room. I finally gave in to having the operation, did my research on surgeons, and now I want to know what in the hell is going on.

"Cody." She clears her throat, avoiding eye contact. "Cody Sterling, right?"

I nod like a goddamn fool. So many thoughts race through my head. She damn well knows my name, but it seems that I'm still tongue-tied.

"Well, I hate to inform you that your surgeon suffered a massive heart attack last night. He's recovering right now but will be unable to perform any surgeries in the near future."

I don't miss the fact Bertie doesn't take it upon herself to sit in the chair in my room or near my bed. Nope—she has one foot in the room and the other one out, as if she's ready to run any moment now.

"Okay," I manage to get out.

"I'll be taking all surgeries in his absence."

"You're a surgeon?" I grit my teeth the second the dumbass question leaves the tip of my tongue.

"Yep." She smirks then blows her loose bangs from her face. "It's not Halloween, Cody, and even if it was, I quit dressing up years ago."

She did it. Damn, my girl really did it, are the only thoughts that race through my head—on repeat. Bertie had a passion for learning. She was bound and determined to become a doctor. Back in the day, she wasn't sure what field she wanted to study. From day to day, she'd drift from wanting to be a vet, scientist, and then would come right back to a doctor. I always teased her that even if she did become a doctor, that I'd have her ass in a sexy, naughty nurse outfit cooking dinner for me. That would ensure a hot and heated make-out session.

"Okay," I stutter out.

"Due to scheduling conflicts, I won't be able to get you into the operating room until tomorrow morning. The hospital will be compensating you for this delay." She taps her iPad one more time, not making eye contact. "Unfortunately, you'll have to fast once again, starting at nine tonight. You will be the first surgery in the morning."

"Stop." I raise my hand, bringing her to an abrupt stop. Finally, she glances up at me, and I find myself speechless once again for a few brief seconds. "Bertie, it's you. It's really you."

Her true emotions shine through for only a few seconds before her mask of indifference reappears.

"Is this how we are going to do it?" I ask, standing to avoid the tug and pull of the tubes and stifling the muffle of the pain that wants to escape as my hip creaks and cracks.

She sighs, tucks her iPad under her arm, and gives me the full force of her stare. It's powerful, just like it was back in the day. She has me hypnotized and eating out of the palm of her hand in a matter of seconds.

"Yes, it is, Cody." She takes a step closer, allowing a familiar scent to attack me. It's the same one from years ago. I'm trapped in a damn time vortex. Coconut Kissing Lime will always be my favorite. "I'm the surgeon that will be performing your surgery tomorrow. End of story."

"Bullshit," I grit out.

Her temper flares as she closes the distance between us. Her pointer finger thumps my chest. "You chose to walk away, Cody, and you also thought it best to give me some type of bullshit excuse. What was it?"

She taps her chin for a few beats.

"Oh, that's right." Her eyes grow big. "We both had different wants and dreams, and our paths would never be the same. And you even had the nerve to get all teary-eyed and shit. It was well-played."

"Bertie." I don't have another chance to get a word out before she's going off in my face again.

"Don't worry, you coward. Bethany had the audacity to tell me what really happened. And I'm smart enough to put two and two together. Let's see how did the story fold out?" She backs up.

"Oh, that's right, I had to study for my first college exam. You wanted to party. I mean, big shocker that Cody Sterling wanted to party. I told you to go and that we would go to the first home football game the next day. Then Cody drank too much and fucked my dorm neighbor and friend, Bethany. Didn't have the balls to tell me the truth, kicked me to the curb, and dropped out of college the next day, leaving the so-called love of his life behind without a second thought."

"I didn't…" Again, I'm cut off.

"Save it. I'm your surgeon and will see you in the

morning." With that, she whirls around, her messy blonde hair following the same action as she disappears out of the room.

My jaw is still slack and open, wanting nothing more than words to spill, but it never happens. I flop back on the bed more desperate than ever. And to think that minutes ago, I was dreading cancer or being told I had weeks to live... This is worse than either of those scenarios.

Chapter 4

Cody

Chocolate pudding can go straight to hell. If I never see that shit again, I would be a happy man. I have no idea who the last nurse was and don't give two shits. I was thankful when she allowed me to sit upright in a chair in my room. The same monotonous beeps and chatter echo from the hallway.

Max and Jessie called a couple of times. I told them what happened with my surgeon but didn't tell them who is now my new surgeon. That piece of the screwed-up puzzle is a part I'm not ready to process.

The seconds feel like hours and the hours feel like an eternity as I stare at the ceiling or the hospital wall. I pick up the journal and read the lyrics; I'd even put pen to paper and found myself slamming it back down. Not even the sweetest song could bring back the flicker of hope I held for years.

I tap my toes on the tile, thinking about the word "redemption," knowing damn well it will never grace my life. I chuckle out loud. The sun has long gone to sleep with the darkness of the night seeping into my room. I've managed to make it through the day. My nerves have flared, and I'm two seconds from checking myself out. I could get a hotel and wait until Jessie or Max could pick me up. It would be a selfish dick move and one I refuse to do. I thought my world spinning, being drunk as fuck at my bar, was hell. That's was a funny joke. This right here is the worst. I steady my arms, deciding to leave and never look back when I'm distracted.

"Mom, Mom." A tiny voice shrills above the dull noise of the hospital.

Then a red ball bounces into my room. I watch the playground-type ball bounce once then twice before it rests underneath my bed.

The hell? I'm done trying to think out my next step. I'm ready to get fixed and the hell out of this place. Bertie made it clear she wanted nothing to do with me, and I have to be okay with that. I don't want to be, but I have no other choice. She laid everything out on the line. I had no clue she knew about me and Bethany. Thing is she's only heard one side of the story, and everyone knows there are always two sides and that the truth lies in the middle. Determined beyond belief, I have to get over the fact my side will never be told.

Tiny blonde, bouncing curls hurricane into my room. It's the first time the attention isn't on me. The small figure is laser-focused on the red ball wedged under my bed.

"Shoot." She slams her balled-up fists on her hips. "This sucks."

She slaps her hand over her mouth and whips her head back. I'm assuming she's making sure her parents didn't hear her. She acts fast, falling to her belly and wiggling under the bed.

"Where did you go?" A voice floats into my room.

It all happens so damn fast I find myself falling back into my chair with my vision darting side to side. Shit, I need to get my head on straight.

"In room four-hundred-four, Mom. I lost my ball," the angelic voice sings out from under the bed.

Visions of more blonde hair whip into my room. It's Bertie. And this time her attention isn't on me. Nope, it's on the tiny body under my bed.

"How many times have I told you that you can't do this?"

"Millions," the tiny girl replies. "Got it, Mom."

Bertie bends down, adjusting her large bag on shoulder, and then wraps her hands around the little girl's ankles. "Ready?"

"Yep, Mom. This is the best ball ever!"

Bertie shakes her head before tugging the little one out. The mini replica of Bertie glides along the hospital floor on her belly with the red ball firmly squeezed between her fingertips.

"Phew." She drops one hand for a second, wiping her hair from her face before clutching the ball again. "I won this today because Miss Teacher said I was the bestest in the class all day long."

"Best," Bertie corrects the little girl.

And in the blink of an eye, Bertie realizes what room she's in. Her face goes pale as we make eye contact.

"Co-Come on, sweetie. You can't run into a

patient's room."

"I know, Mom." The little girl with bright blonde hair and big eyes clutches the ball to her chest. "I promised you I wouldn't do it again, but I was finally good. So, so good. I wanted to punch Belle in the face and spit on Lilly, but I didn't, Mom, and won this." She throttles the ball up in the air.

Bertie smiles. It's genuine and raw, and I haven't seen something that beautiful in years.

"Okay, tell Co-this patient sorry."

The little girl whips my direction. "Sorry."

I nod. "No worries."

Bertie clutches the top of the little girl's shoulder as the tiny one glances around the room. "I'm really sorry. This shouldn't have happened."

Bertie's cheeks flush a bright red. She doesn't have to speak a word that she wasn't willing to give me this piece of her life, but that damn red ball did. Red may be my new favorite color.

I wave her off. "Just staring at the walls. It's no big deal, really."

"Do you need anything?" She checks her Apple Watch on her wrist. "I can't get you a pizza or any food, but maybe a word search or something."

I'd give anything to freeze this moment. Bertie is talking to me again as if I were a human. I'd give anything to relive this moment over and over again.

"Word search!" The little girl jumps up and down. "Mom, can we do one?"

My breath hitches deep in my chest. This little girl is something else. It's only been a few minutes, and I know this beyond a doubt. Bertie Cooper has a daughter who is her complete opposite. Wild and carefree in every way. Before I have the time to process the fact that Bertie may be married or have an ex, a shrill scream bounces off the walls of my hospital room.

"That's my name." She points her chubby finger at the sign detailing my room number, name, who my nurse is, what room I'm in, and the last time I pissed. "Mom, that's my name."

Bertie bites her bottom lip, not as thrilled as her daughter, and that's the moment she breaks our eye contact, dropping her gaze to her shoes. They tap the ground in sync as my thundering heart threatens to shatter my rib cage.

"I'm Cody." The tiny one beats her chest.

I raise an eyebrow, speaking before thinking which is my norm. "No, I'm Cody."

She bounds my way, escaping Bertie's grasp. "You are a boy, and your name is Cody?"

Her giggles fill my heart as she slaps her hand over her mouth. "You have a girl name."

I shrug and lift my arms out to the side. "You got me. My mom gave me a dam…" I clear my throat, "…a darn girl name."

"That sucks, dude." She wrinkles her nose.

"Cody." Bertie's stern voice cuts into our conversation. "What have I told you about that word?"

"It's yucky and sounds yucky and only yucky people say it."

Bertie shakes her head. "Not quite, but that will do."

"Roberta." A booming voice cuts into our moment.

"In here," she responds.

Moments later, a tall man with blond hair enters the room. If it weren't for his suit, I'd guess he was a beach bum with his dark tan and dazzling white smile. He checks the Rolex on his wrist before glancing up.

"We have thirty minutes before we are late for our dinner date."

"Mom, no!" Cody stomps her foot. "I don't wanna have to stay with that mean lady. She only watches the news, and I have to keep my back straight."

I don't miss the man's jaw clenching and Bertie struggling to remedy the situation. She ushers her daughter back to her side and whispers something in her ear. The man I decide to call "Doctor Dickweed" pulls a large diamond ring out of his pocket.

"You can change at Mom's house when we drop her off, but put this on now." He slides the enormous rock on her finger.

The pieces fall together—the epic proposals. Doctor Dickweed has my girl. The bottom of my world falls out. I clench my jaw tight, wanting nothing more than to stand up and whip this dickhead's ass. It's not my place. I lost her. My actions proved this fact.

"Hey," I holler out.

Little Cody turns around, all of her excitement now gone.

"Nice meeting you, Cody 2.0." I wink at her.

This gains me a grin.

She shakes her head, clutching her red ball to her chest. "You have a girl name."

I nod my head. "Guess I do."

"We need to go or we'll be late." Doctor Dickweed clutches Bertie's arm, tugging her along, her mini-me following right behind them, gracing me with her smile the entire time.

Even though I'm sitting down in a chair, my world spins faster than a merry-go-round. I'm lost for words or thoughts. Britt's comment about the epic proposal ricochets. She wasn't a fan. I wasn't a fan the moment the man entered the room. The mood changed faster than I could blink. It's one of those times when you know nothing, but poison is about to seep into your blood.

Bertie has a little girl. She can't be a day over five or six. The timeline doesn't add up for her being mine, but that doesn't mean a damn thing. She's so pure and amazing. By the time I manage to get back into my bed with all the damn tubes and shit in place, my mind reels with all the what-ifs and could-have-beens.

Chapter 5

Cody

My eyelids are heavy as the nurses wheel me down to the operating room. Ceiling tiles and dim lights pass one by one. All through the night, I wasn't able to process a damn thing, let alone that the hands of the woman I love are about to fix my body.

I nod when nurses tell me things and even ask me questions. It's a fantastic and haunting blur. I'm left in a tiny room wrapped in warm blankets, minutes from heading into the operating room.

"Mr. Sterling." I'd recognize that voice anywhere. I sit up in my bed, coming eye to eye with Bertie. "Just wanted to stop by and see if you had any questions."

"You named her Cody," ghosts off my lips.

"I'm here to do a job. How are you feeling? Do you have any questions?"

"Bertie." I grab for her hand, but she steps back faster than I can reach her.

"Cody, the past is just that. Leave it there. You made your choice years ago. Hell, more than a decade ago. Leave it there." She crosses her arms. "Unless you have any questions, I'll see you in a few in the operating room."

"Don't do this," I plead. I'm a desperate man, yearning just for a morsel of the past.

"I'm engaged. I'm in love with a damn good man. There's nothing here to discuss, Cody. We were once fools in love, or what we thought love was."

I shake my head. "You know it was more than that, and you don't love him."

She steps closer, leaning over my bed. "I do. In fact, I do with everything I have. He's a good man who would never do what you did to me."

"I didn't sleep with her."

"Yeah." She crosses her arms over her chest, and even though her blonde locks are hidden by the scrub hat on the top of her head, she looks sexy as hell.

"I didn't. She tried. Took me to her room. I thought you were going to be there. You weren't. We kissed, and I passed out." I cringe at the words coming out of my mouth, but they need to be said. "I was piss drunk, and she was hell bent on having me. No excuses, Bertie. You deserve the truth."

She nods her head. "Thanks for the truth, years later. Again, I'm engaged to a man who would never do such things. Cody, there's not even a chance of friendship for us. If you don't have any questions, everything is on track for a successful surgery." She raises an eyebrow.

I shake my head. "I'm still flesh and bones. Bertie, I'm human. I've fucked up and can admit to it. You could at least treat me like one."

"All right, then, see you in a bit." With that, she turns her stiffened spine on me and walks right out of the tiny holding room.

The warm blankets do nothing with the frosty chill she just sent through me. I have no idea how anyone would react in this situation, but this would be the worst option.

***

Bertie

I square my shoulders as I scrub up, repeating to myself over and over again, "This is just another operation." I've performed hundreds of hip replacements. Hell, I could do it in my sleep. It doesn't matter how many times I tell myself it's the same; I know this is different.

I've known the reason he gave me a piss-poor excuse years ago. Bethany was all too proud to shove it in my face. Her story was exaggerated to the nines. I knew this, but you know what they say about the imagination.

I deflected back to my point of safety, telling him over and over I was in love with Garrett. It's the furthest from the truth. He nailed me at a weak point, and I said yes. Cody doesn't need to know that, and I'll convince my heart it isn't true until I believe it. I don't get it right all the time, but this time I will.

I told Garrett about Cody. Well, I gave him a very watered-down version as in we went to high school together. I pleaded my case to the higher-ups that I shouldn't be doing this surgery. They didn't care. They needed bodies and things to flow like normal with one surgeon out.

I don't enter the OR like I typically do and smile down kindly to the patient, letting them know they're in safe hands before they drift off to sleep. I don't have it in me. I can't face him. He's the one man who holds the power to shred me from limb to limb. Everything I forced myself to spew at him was a damn lie. I still love him and always will. And that's one secret I'll never let him in on.

"Roberta Cooper, you're strong, smart, and got this," I whisper to myself.

It isn't the first time I've had this sentiment running through my mind. In fact, it was my mantra when Cody left me, the day Cody reentered my world, and every day since.

"He's ready," my nurse announces.

My favorite song, "Say You Love Me" by Fleetwood Mac, begins humming through the chilled room as I enter. I find myself swaying back and forth, making my way to the patient, never glancing at his face. Call me a coward, because that's what I am with the way I just treated him.

I crossed boundaries allowing a personal past to enter the present, but I refuse to allow it to mess with my head. It was all lies I spit at him. Falling for Cody Sterling again would be the easiest thing I could ever do. Hell, I named my daughter after him, hoping like hell it would grace her with his zest and live-out-loud gusto for life.

My team nods, knowing it's go time. I even find a smile gracing my lips, remembering all the times

Cody would hold me as he screwed up the words to this song. He always knew it was my favorite. And it's always been the song that's played in my operating room. It was my foundation, like the man lying on my operating table.

Once again I square my shoulders. This man I'm about to operate on saved me when I was lost in this big bad world. He was the one who encouraged me to be the person I am deep down. Hell, he bragged about his sexy little nerd in front of the entire town. There wasn't a moment he wasted not letting me know how much he loved me.

He may have broken my heart, but by damn, I will mend this broken man. I have no idea why a guy his age would be in this shape, but it's none of my business. With one last hip sway and bob of my head, I gear my team into action. I don't miss the horrific burns on his leg and force myself to ignore them.

With the first slice, I'm taken back into history, feeling his arms wrapped around me as he sways me to this song. I've never been so in the zone before. It's like magic.

I will never be able to give Cody Sterling my heart again, but I will give him this. My hands move automatically as I perform each step. I don't miss the fact that each song that plays overhead brings back a memory or dozen of the love of my life, Cody. He's always been the playlist of my life.

The monitors begin buzzing. Frantic action ensues as Cody flatlines right beneath my hands. My mind whirls and whizzes for a few beats.

"Cooper!" My name echoes around the sterile, chilled room followed by other words, but I'm unable to process them.

I glance up at the monitor, seeing the flatline, and have no idea what in the hell is happening.

I'm shoved out of the way by my intern, who hollers for the paddles. All I can do is stare down at my blood-covered gloves. I swear nothing makes sense. His labs were excellent, he's healthy, he may drink a bit too much, but he's in great shape. It all reels through my mind in slow motion. The movie of my life. The what could have been and what never did lies before me with no heartbeat.

I'm unable to process or even move. I watch as my team hollers out, doing their best to save Cody's life. All I can do is stand there and watch the love of my life drift away. The taste of bitterness that slipped off my song is now bathed on his soul. It will be the last message he ever heard from me.

Chapter 6

Bertie

I flip page after page of Cody's records, getting no closer to understanding what happened in the OR. All I do know is that I froze, ignoring all my instincts as a surgeon. That has never happened before. My team used the paddles, bringing Cody back to life. With only a few steps left, I was able to finish the surgery. But now he's in a bed in the ICU, fighting for his life.

My eyes glance over all the labs and his medical history; not one thing makes sense. By all means, the information in front of me shows he should have been the easiest surgery ever, including his recovery time. Cody should be up and walking now after the sedation wore off. But instead he's on a ventilator in ICU. He never woke up after he was brought back to life. The machines are doing everything for the most charismatic man I've ever known. Nobody is as full of life as is the Cody from all my memories. I can see life has been hard on him.

I slam down his labs then toss my iPad at the wall. Even the Chief of Surgery told me I did nothing wrong and sometimes things can't be explained. Didn't help that it's Garrett, and he spent a whole whopping thirty seconds on the damn conversation. My intern is buried under a pile of books and paperwork, scouring for an answer because that's all I want.

Garrett, my fiancé, couldn't give a shit less. It shouldn't matter whether I know the patient or not. He should be concerned that a life flatlined under my hands. That's his job to be there to support me. I settled with him as my boyfriend and now future husband. I won't settle with him as the Chief of Surgery.

After hours of poring through the same damn test results, I give up and walk out of the stale room where surgeons get the chance to relax. My feet are weighed down with dead mass as I walk to the elevator and push the button to his floor. The inside of the elevator suffocates me as tears slip from the corners of my eyes. The elevator creeps inch by inch as my heart continues to break. I feel like shit. Lower than low…it's worse than the day Cody walked away, the day Bethany told me what happened in her terms, and even more earth-shattering the day I found I was expecting a little life. I have no words.

I can't even begin to understand why I'm going to see him. My body is on auto-pilot, seeking him out. It's the only place I want to be. I brush away the tears as soon as the doors open and use my work badge to enter the ICU. I don't make eye contact with anyone as I make my way to his room.

I freeze for a second before sliding open the glass door. I don't recognize Cody. The man lying in the bed is far from the man I once knew. I tug the chair closer to his bedside, grab his hand, squeezing it tight for my own comfort, and drop my head. The tears turn on without warning, flowing down without regret.

"I'm sorry. I'm so damn sorry, Cody." I can't even make out the muffled words that escape from me. "I was so mean to you. So, so mean. I was protecting myself from you. Because you, Cody, have always owned me and are the one man with enough power to destroy me."

I go on and on, telling him everything, pleading with him to fight for his next breath. Once my throat is hoarse and I'm exhausted, I pull out my phone and find the playlist. Our playlist that I've listened to thousands of times and never tired of.

The music plays low and soft, hugging both of us with its lyrics. I find myself singing along to each song. The variety of the playlist ranges from Charley Pride to Beyonce. "When Fast Car" by Tracy Chapman begins playing, the tears appear again. It was our song. Cody always promised me he'd take me away in a fast car to any university I wanted to study at. I'd give anything right now to give him a fast car taking away all of his problems.

I close my eyes, watching the movie of our memories flash by while a sliver of hope builds inside me, wanting to make more memories with this man. I can't. It's the raw emotion racing through me. I check the time and know I have to leave now in order to pick up Cody from her dance class in thirty minutes.

I stand, wiping away the stray tears and mess from my face. I have no doubt wiping away the tears does little to erase the evidence of my sorrow. My eyes are puffy and cheeks heated, not to mention my stuffy nose. Light beeping serenades the hall of the ICU with nurses quietly checking charts and patients. I manage to make it out into the waiting room, not running into anyone. That is a miracle in itself.

I hear a friendly, familiar voice when I enter the waiting room, not thinking straight enough to take the back route to avoid people. My best friend and fellow surgeon, Trent McCray, sits on a worn chair with his elbows resting on top of his thighs in a gentle fashion. He rushed into my OR after he finished up a surgery of his own for moral support and to help finish up Cody's procedure. And now he's talking to…

I glance up to the group of people and immediately notice Jessie and Brady in the small crowd. They were Cody's best friends from high school and amazing guys. But the grief dancing in their eyes have me damn near crumbling right back down.

"Bertie." Jessie rises to his feet, scrubbing the stubble on his jaw. "What are you doing here?"

Before he finishes his question, I know he's answered himself by the way his brows crunch up. A woman sitting next to him with long, thick, wavy brown hair stands by his side with red, swollen eyes gripping his arm. It takes me a few beats to recognize Jules, Jessie's high school sweetheart, until one day

43

they were no more.

"It was you?" he seethes. "No wonder his heart quit beating."

"Jessie," Jules hisses.

Trent is on his feet, standing between me and the crowd. "Doctor Cooper is one of the best surgeons here. There's no need for this."

Brady yanks Jessie back and finally makes eye contact. The hurt and sorrow playing out in his caring eyes guts me. He gifts me with a jerk of a chin and doesn't say a damn thing.

I go to open my mouth, but nothing comes out. I've learned over the years that at times it's best to say nothing at all. And this is certainly one of those. I bite down on my bottom lip, stare at my clogs that still have a dabble of Cody's blood on them, and begin to walk away, feeling the weight of the world on my shoulders.

"Walk away. That's what you do best." Jessie's voice echoes around the suffocating waiting room.

His words strike me dead center in the heart. I freeze, turn to him, darting my angry gaze right at him. I've been ripped in so many different directions the past twenty-four hours, lines have been blurred, while I've been drowning in the murky color grey. There hasn't been a single ounce of black and white.

"Rich words coming from you, Jessie. Seems you perfected walking away." I square my shoulders, not able to handle one more damn thing today.

"Bertie," Trent warns.

I completely ignore him, not willing to be put down by a stranger from my past who has no idea what he's talking about.

"You have no idea. I did nothing wrong, and if you feel otherwise, I suggest you shut your mouth and file a complaint with the hospital. I will not tolerate being put down by the likes of you."

It's brutal honesty. I internally wince at my own words but don't regret them. I'm punishing myself enough and don't need his shit right now, or in fact, ever. The room falls silent, and I don't wait for a response before marching out of the room and into the staff room.

I pound my fist into the front of my locker, dropping my forehead to it, feeling defeated. My once-sturdy world that was planted firmly below my feet is now spinning faster than a rollercoaster, making me dizzy as hell. It's the same feeling I experienced when Cody Sterling first smirked and sidled up to me in English class. Same feeling, totally different circumstances, with one common denominator. Cody.

I slide down to the floor, nursing my throbbing fist to my chest. The door creaks open, but I don't look up.

"On your feet, Cooper." Trent kneels down, bringing up my chin with his finger. "We all have days like this, and you're not going to let it take you down."

"How? What the hell happened? What did I do wrong?" My chin begins to quiver.

"Stop. You did nothing wrong. I reviewed the charts too. I don't have an answer for you, babe." He cups my cheek. "What I do know is that I'm going to kick your ass if you fall. Dust it off. He's alive."

Before I know it, Trent grabs my hand and pulls

me to my feet. He does his best, reminding me of everything I have and the reasons to move forward. He leaves out Garrett, and that's no surprise. Trent is not a fan of the man.

"Dry those tears, quit being a baby, and go get that perfect little girl of yours." He slaps my ass.

"He's the one, Trent. It's Cody lying in that bed up in the ICU. The man I've always loved who flatlined under my hands."

"Yeah, I know." He pulls open my locker and begins stuffing my shit in my oversized bag. "You never should've been operating on him because of that. But seems Doctor Douchebag couldn't care less."

"Don't." I raise my hand, cutting off Trent's rant on Garrett before he can even warm up.

Trent has been by my side throughout internship and residency, and now we work at the same hospital. He's a cardiac surgeon while I went to orthopedics. He's the typical manwhore, best friend, and has dead-on senses. Every single time I chose to ignore his warnings, I found myself on the losing side. But when it came to Garrett, I was simply lonely and enjoyed his companionship in the beginning. As time wore on, the real man behind the mask made his appearance. Our relationship morphed into him showing me off on his arm, flaunting his money with the stupid engagement ring, and being a smug asshole.

"Here." Trent slaps the huge diamond ring into my palm like it is searing his skin.

I wiggle it on my finger, too damn exhausted to dissect what the hell I am going to do. I give him a quick peck on the cheek before making my way out of the locker room.

"Give my girl a squeeze and kiss for me." Trent winks.

"Will do."

The sun has already begun its fall to slumber. Oranges and pink hues blaze all over the parking lot. I click the key fob to my practical, mid-size SUV, concentrating on my footsteps, hoping like hell I can completely redo this entire day.

"Roberta." A voice echoes around me, and a shrill of chills race up my spine. Only one person calls me that name, and he only does it because it sounds more sophisticated than Bertie. I despise it.

I turn to see Garrett jogging up to me in his three-piece suit, his thick hair perfectly in place.

"Hey, baby." He kisses my forehead. His lips feel like sandpaper on my skin as my back grows ramrod straight. "Did you forget about our dinner tonight?"

I tilt my head to the side, biting down on my bottom lip. My weakness is overreacting when I'm physically exhausted. This fact I learned over the last few years. I can't imagine how I'd be when I was emotionally exhausted as well. I mull my words through my sluggish brain before stringing together a sentence.

"I don't remember a dinner date, Garrett." I don't even miss the venom lacing each word.

"I texted you today at lunch."

And I detonate like a ticking time bomb. Red blurs my vision with no end in sight.

"Excuse me?" I adjust my bag on my shoulder and shove his chest, the tip of my key piercing the inside of my palm. The pain fuels me on. "You texted me."

"Hey now." He holds his hands up in the air. "Calm down. You can get dressed at home and I'll pick you up. We have about forty-five minutes."

"You are unbelievable." I shake my head and turn away, knowing this will go nowhere. The man doesn't show one ounce of empathy for what I've gone through today.

"It's with a large pharmaceutical company and at your favorite steak place on the canyon."

I rip open my car door, toss in my bag and keys, then slip the diamond ring from my finger, taking three sure steps his way.

"Here, take this and enjoy your fucking dinner. And for your information, Taco Time is my favorite place to eat but clearly below you." I go to whirl around but have more to say and don't stop until I get it all out. "I needed you today, Garrett, and you weren't there. I told you I didn't want to be in on that operation. You couldn't give two shits."

"Roberta, you're overreacting." He reaches out a hand, and I bat it away.

"No, I'm not. You're a self-centered asshole, Garrett, and I'm done being your toy."

"No." His jaw tightens. "We are engaged. The whole hospital knows this."

"And tomorrow they'll know we are not."

"Listen." He grabs my hips before I can move back again. "I've been overwhelmed with the new position and all the pressure. You're right. I should've been there today. I'm so sorry."

He presses his lips to my forehead. It's on the tip of my tongue to tell him he's nowhere the man Cody

48

is, even after what happened between the two of us. I suck my lips in and trap the words.

"Go home, baby. I'll come over after dinner, and we can talk." He slides the ring back on my finger.

My bones and muscles collapse in weariness. I have no more fight lingering in me. I take a step back.

"Okay, but not tonight. I just want to go home and be with Cody. She's what I need right now."

Garrett shakes his head.

"What?" I demand.

"Nothing." He runs his hand through his hair. "I'll text when I'm done with the dinner."

With that, he turns and strides to his car. The black, sleek one with leather seats. The same one Cody isn't allowed a juice box in and her dog, Scotty, can never ride in. What in the hell have I done?

As soon as I start my car, my cell phone beeps with an incoming text. I look down to see a selfie of my daughter and best friend, Nell, smiling brightly at the camera. Those two can always light up the darkest of days. Pressing my finger on the photo, I save it to my camera roll. I swear those two fill the pictures on my phone. They're a light in the dark, seeing their bright smile.

After saving the pic, I then read her short but to the point text message.

Nell: I picked up Cody meet you at the house. Also grabbed Taco Time for dinner. You know you love me.

I shake my head and find myself smiling for the first time today. Nell is my best friend from college and the only sister I've ever had. We couldn't be any different than two people are. She's a fashion designer while I went to med school. But we were the best two roommates the stars ever aligned.

We were assigned to be dorm partners our first year and never left each other's sides. Nell's fashion career and lifestyle blog can operate anywhere, and that's why we are still neighbors. Idaho really isn't the best location for her, but she makes it work.

She's Cody's godmother and my favorite person in this world. On the short drive to my house, I find myself feeling lighter than I have all day. Yes, Cody flatlined under my hands. But he's alive and will be off the ventilator in a few days when he comes out of his coma.

Chills race over my skin as I pull into my small one-car garage. I vow right here and now to erase the thoughts of the day into a distant memory. Or at least that's what I tell myself.

When I enter the house, it's full-on chaos, and I knew it would be that way with Nell and Cody in charge. Scotty, the naughtiest Chihuahua on the face of the world, races around the house, barking his high-pitched squeal. Cody chases him, still wearing her little tutu from dance class, and the whole time Nell perches on my couch, eating a taco and sipping from a glass of wine.

I shake my head and find myself laughing at the scene before me then grab a taco from the greasy brown bag on the counter. Nell already has a glass of wine poured for me as I plop down on the couch next to her, propping my feet on the coffee table.

Typically, seeing all the stuffing from one of

Scotty's plush toys spread all over the floor would piss me off. Not tonight. I actually find myself smiling at the mess, appreciating the value of life and what I have.

"What's up with you?" Nell takes a huge bite out of her taco.

"Long, horrible day." I pause, but Nell doesn't accept that as an answer. After my first swallow of a delicious cheesy crunchy taco, I tell her everything.

She knows who Cody is. She was there with me through all of it. Bethany roomed next to us in the towers but was always hanging out with us. She didn't fit in, and Nell knew it from the time we all met. I was more naïve and gave the girl a chance; looking back, it was the biggest mistake of my life. Cody may have screwed up, but I sure in the hell didn't do anything to try to protect our relationship.

Nell falls silent, since there are no words to even offer a glimpse of sympathy. I'm thankful that she knows me so well. A simple pat on the leg while pouring me another glass of wine is all I need to know.

"And there's more," I admit then take a sip of the crisp, sweet white wine, glancing over at Cody, who has dozed off on her oversized pillow with Naughty Scotty cuddled up to her side. "Garrett."

Nell groans, rolls her eyes, and bites down on her lip. "I'll just listen, because you know my opinion."

"Yeah, same as Trent's. You've two made it damn well known. I don't need it right now. I was an idiot. I swear."

"Keep going." Nell tops off my half glass of wine. "Spit it out. We've done dumb things."

51

I rake my hand through my hair. "I do feel something for Garrett. The thing is, as the days go by, it's as if his true colors show through more and more."

She nods, encouraging me to continue.

"He chased me out of the hospital tonight, insisting I'd be late for our dinner date, which I had no damn clue about. I swear he thinks I'm just his play toy. He had no remorse, and not even an ounce of sympathy for what I went through today, not as my boss and sure in the hell not as my supposed fiancé. Long story shorter. I gave him back the engagement ring."

This causes Nell to perk up. I now have her whole interest. "Go on," she urges.

"He did what Garrett does and tried to smooth it over. He put it back on my finger."

I don't miss the fact she grimaces and looks like she's ready to bare her teeth and growl at me.

"I threw it in my purse before I drove home. I'm so lost. I swear, one moment life was good. I have this parent and work combo thing down. Thought I was falling in love again with a good guy and boom, shit hit the fan."

"I really tried here, Bertie, but I have to give my two cents." Nell relaxes on the couch. "Garrett is a good-looking man. He played you well in the beginning, but you're right, his true colors are showing through. The thing I can't take and I know you can't either is how he treats her." She nudges her head in the direction of Cody, who is stirring and causing Scotty to grumble at her. "He has never once acknowledged the importance of your own daughter in his life or yours. He treats her like a dirty little secret, and it's complete bullshit. The only reason I haven't blown up so far is because you make up for masking his discontent with her. But is that how you really envision the rest of your life?"

And there it is, the punch straight to the gut that I needed. She smacked the nail on the head with every point. At first, I thought Garrett was uncomfortable around kids, so I did my best to introduce the two and ended up overcompensating for the way Garrett treats her. It's all just so screwed up.

"And you don't have to answer that." She stands, patting my shoulder. "I know you're a better person than to want your life like that. I'm crashing on the couch after I steal your favorite blanket. Love ya, like a bad case of a contagious rash or hives or whatever the hell."

A light chuckle escapes. I can't but think of all our wine-drunk stunts, and we are about another swallow or two before that happens again. Exhaustion has overwhelmed me; I have a cute, perfect little girl, and an asshole dog that's calling my name.

"'Night," I whisper after a dozen tacos had been consumed between the two of us, nearly two bottles of wine downed, and my imaginary white surrender flag waves high in the air.

Scotty bares his teeth at me and does his best version of a menacing growl when I scoop Cody up in my arms, which causes him to roll off her side. I really thought it was a cute and clever idea to adopt a puppy when Cody turned four. Little did I know, we were adopting the puppy of Satan. If there's a trash can to dive in, a sound to bark at, or a piece of carpet to piss on, Scotty is your dog. As big of a pain in the ass as he is, he owns a piece of my heart. He lets Cody do anything to him from dressing him up to painting his toenails. The damn dog idolizes her.

Just like Garrett should, I think to myself.

Nell already has herself burrito wrapped in my favorite fluffy blanket and is passed out flat on the couch. I shake my head and smile, feeling right at home in my own house. That's the feeling I crave to get high on and must ground myself to.

"Momma," Cody grumbles as I force her to tug on her favorite sunshine yellow pajamas when all I want to do is collapse in the yellow blankets covering her bed.

"Yeah, baby." I brush back her bouncy yellow curls.

"I didn't get in trouble today."

"Good girl." I kiss the tip of her nose while tugging her top down in place.

"Nell is right." Her eyes go bright and wide as she hits full wide-awake mode.

"What do you mean?" I ask, ripping my bra off and wiggling into some comfy clothes, keeping everything tucked in. I'm a black belt in this art and have it down to less than ten seconds, wine drunk or not.

"Garrett is mean. He doesn't like me. And I know I'm dumb, but he's mean, Mom."

I tug down the hem of my favorite t-shirt as her last words pierce my heart. I stare my wide-eyed girl in the eye and get real. Because if this world has taught me anything, it's that you have to be real or it will swallow you whole.

"He's an asshole, sweetie. There's no way to sugarcoat it." And with a stern look, I tell her the most important part. "I never want to hear you say that again. You are not dumb, Cody girl. You're brilliant, talented, and the most loving girl I know."

"Thanks, Momma." She wipes the sleep from her eyes and spreads her arms wide.

I swoop her from the counter and carry her to her bed, making sure to tuck her in on her favorite side before cuddling up behind her. It's perfect. Besides, I don't have my favorite blanket, and that's truly nothing in the scheme of things.

Cody snuggles up next to me. Her sweet breath tickles the flesh under my chin like a fresh rain, each droplet a promise of forever that I'll never forget.

"Mom."

"Yeah, Cody." I know she's wide awake now: she calls me Mom and not Momma.

"We didn't say goodnight to Dad."

I tap her nose. "You're right."

I roll over, flick on the lamp, and bring the framed photo to her. "You're the smartest girl I know." I tuck the photo between us.

"Night, Dad. I love you so, so, so much. I hope you're having fun in heaven and taking care of Goldie the fish."

Cody reaches up, pressing her lips to the glass and squeezing her eyes shut. I don't have to ask to know she's making a wish all her own.

Garrett wouldn't have any time for this nonsense.

Cody Sterling, on the other hand, would cherish every moment, even though his namesake isn't his.

Chapter 7

Bertie

"Mom." Cody plops a syrup-drenched waffle piece in her mouth. "Can I get hot pink boots when my star chart fills up?"

Nell winces at what I assume is Cody's loud voice then ruffles her ponytail. "You hate pink, squirt."

Cody shrugs. "Lilly, the one with all the friends, loves pink and…"

"Whoa," I round the counter after setting down my glass of orange juice, "that doesn't mean you have to like pink."

She dips her head, staring at her dangling feet. "It will make me smarter."

"Honey." I grab her and hug her tight to my chest. The drumming pain in my chest strikes an ache I've never felt before. It's my wake-up call: I have a struggling little girl right in front of me, one who is insecure and struggling to fit into the mainstream of the world. I was there once, until one crazy boy entered my life. And damn if I'm going to make my Cody wait that long. It's time I put my life back in order right now.

"Screw pink. It's a color and not yours. You never have to wear or like something because it's popular." I hold her tight to my chest. "Wear yellow and rock it, baby girl. And what did I tell you?" I don't wait for her response repeating the same sentiment again to her and will do it for the rest of my days until she believes it. "Cody girl, you're brilliant, talented, and the most-loving girl I know."

"Yeah." Nell slams down her coffee mug and winces. "You wear yellow, scream yellow, and rock the shit out of it. You make yellow the best damn color until Lilly loves it."

We spend the rest of the morning doing our best damn girl jam getting Cody ready for school. Garrett blew up my phone all morning, and I ignored every single message he sent.

Clutching the diamond ring in my palm, I walk into the break room, burning with passion. Not the same passion I once thought this piece of jewelry would bring in my life; it's disgust and anger that I nearly tumbled down that rabbit hole.

I was relieved to find out that I was taken off all surgeries today and only have to do rounds. To say I was shocked is an understatement; I never thought Garrett would get a clue. I tap my foot impatiently, waiting for him to enter the vacant break room. It's probably not the best time to do this, but really, when is it ever?

The door bursts open, and Garrett rushes in, revealing his notorious and glorious frazzled state.

It's sexy on him, with his perfect features tensed and shoulders strung tight. It takes me back to the first time I fell for him.

"Hey." He closes the distance between us with his large palm grabbing my hip, tugging me to him.

I wince at the overwhelming fruity smell emanating off him. I wrinkle my nose and take a step back. Neon fuchsia fills my vision, a pink so bright it turns my stomach until bile burns the back of my throat. Without thinking, I reach up and strum the pink-hued stain on Garrett's collar.

He glances down at the action then covers my hand with his, squeezing it gently.

"Who was she?" I whisper, not making eye contact.

He presses his lips to the top of my head, gifting me a tender kiss. "You know my mom loves her pink lipstick."

"And the smell?" I squeeze my eyes shut, having no idea if I'm relieved or disgusted by him right now.

"She got a new perfume," he offers.

I push back from him, squeezing the ring tighter in my grip until the sharp edges pierce the inside of my palm. I eye him up and down, not having to ask the question out loud.

"I was called in last night. Haven't had a chance to change. Long-ass night." He takes a step back from me, reading my body language then nervously running his hand through his tousled hair.

"Thank you for taking me off the schedule."

"It's hospital protocol. You'll be off surgeries for the next two weeks."

I nod, knowing that already, and decide I don't

have time in my life to prolong this.

"It's over, Garrett. We aren't working and are definitely blurring lines as it is. We want different things in life." I step up to him. When he doesn't hold his hand out, I place the engagement ring in the pocket in the front of his suit. I give it one gentle and final pat.

"I love being a surgeon. I love working here, and I hope that can continue." I step back and turn from him, glancing over my shoulder. "I wish you no ill will, Garrett."

He remains stoic and silent until my hand is on the door, ready to pull it open.

"Bertie."

I freeze but don't turn around.

"Are you sure about this?"

"Yes." The one word comes out resolute and determined.

"You're going to regret making me look like a fool," he hisses.

This forces me to whirl around. "I don't think threatening an employee is a great idea."

An evil chuckle escapes him, a sound I've never heard from him before. I know staying here and engaging with him is a losing battle.

"You've been warned." Garrett's final volley isn't lost on me.

I knew this wouldn't be easy, yet I don't let it rattle me one bit when I start my day. I'm not going to be a hypocrite when I pumped my daughter full of encouragement this morning about being brave and being herself. Hell no, there's no more time to be a coward. I square my shoulders as I walk down the hall and ride the elevator up to the ICU. I ignore all the pity stares from co-workers.

Doesn't take a fool to know damn well the news and gossip spread about yesterday's operation. For the most part, employees here are professional and respect boundaries. There are always a few rotten seeds.

"Bertie."

I freeze mid-step when I hear my name being called. I whirl around, on high alert. It's natural instinct as my body goes into fight-or-flight mode. I come face-to-face with Jessie James. I turn back around, having nothing to say to him. Damn, I'm checking shitty people off my list one at a time. I know no matter how many times I apologize to him, he'll sling all sorts of shit right back in my face.

"Please listen," he begs.

I don't stop, and he keeps up with me step for step. I don't dare glance sideways at him.

"I want to apologize. I was freaked out yesterday. Cody is like a brother to me, and I was scared shitless."

This causes me to freeze mid-stride. I slowly turn to Jessie, keeping my shoulders squared in confidence. "How do you think I felt? Oh, wait, that doesn't matter, does it?"

I shiver at the harshness of my own words, but it's time I stick up for myself.

"It does, and that's why I'm here. It was a dick move and one I'm not proud of at all. I know words aren't enough." He runs his hands down the scruff of his jawline. "I'm going to be real blunt right now. Seeing you brought back all the memories of how you destroyed Cody, and that's why I reacted. It's a shit excuse. I'm so sorry."

"He never told you, did he?" I shake my head.

"Oh, he did. I've heard about you for years and seen the punishment and pain he put himself through when he let you go." Jessie drops his head. "I've seen him go through hell and survive there."

"He never told you," I repeat.

Jessie scrunches his brows.

"Yeah, he obviously told me the same lie he told all of you. He let me go because our paths were going separate ways. The truth is he got piss drunk and damn near screwed a close friend and practical roommate of mine. That's what happened, Jessie."

Silence pierces the air between us. It's deafening and about to swallow me whole. It's too painful to allow the hurt to crush me under a bed of rubble.

"And none of the past matters. I'd do anything for a patient, not to mention one that's owned my heart since he entered my world." I clutch my scrubs and release them. "If you have any questions, please consult with Trent. He'll take damn good care of you. Have a nice day, Mr. James, and please let us know if we can do anything to make your stay here at the hospital better."

With that, I walk straight toward Cody's room. I turn on our playlist to the lightest sound possible as I enter. The beeps and pumping of the machine way out power the music playing through my phone. But the thing is, the power of our memories and words of the songs trumps everything. My body moves automatically like I'm a fine-oiled robot.

My lips brush along Cody's forehead. The

warmth of his skin brings me comfort as if my favorite childhood blanket and Mom's arms are wrapped around me, cocooning me in safety and love. I'm way past the grey area, swimming deep in black murky pools. The heart wants what the heart wants.

Elvis Presley, Jason Aldean, Tim McGraw, and various other artists revive our past one moment at a time. It's a selfish act, and I relish in the memories of us, the time where I had everything and nothing at the same time. I'm so confused, but all I know is I'm at home when I'm by his side.

The days pass like this then turn into two weeks. Jessie and Jules' visits are less frequent. I'll give it to them—they're tried and true friends making the five-hour drive to be with Cody even though they both have full time jobs and families. Their dedication makes me miss something that's been absent in my life for years. Well, since…Cody. There's no reminiscing about old times. Nope, there's just a slight nod and flat smile exchanged between us.

***

Cody

Son of a bitch. There's black, a flash of white, then a sizzling sensation zapping through my body from the roots of my hair to the tips of my toes. It's pain like I've never experienced before. I thought I knew what pain felt like before. I was so very wrong.

The organ in the middle of my chest that grants me life is sluggish. My muscles don't work like they did before. I have nothing. Absolutely nothing. My throat scratches, and I fight to swallow. There's something there blocking my airway. A siren of beeps and buzzers go off, splitting my head.

My eyelids are heavily weighed down with a ton of cement. The harder I battle to get in a gasp of air, the worse my problem becomes. I'm drowning damn fast in quicksand, and the more I fight to move, the further down I sink.

"Calm down, Cody." A hand lands on my shoulder. "I need you to relax."

I still can't open my eyes, but the words "Fuck off" are on the tip of my tongue. A rush of madness invades what was my peaceful slumber. My eyes shoot open and snap shut in the blink of an eye. The lights in the ceiling blind me with a deathly cloak as pain attacks my body. Every muscle roped in my body tears away. It's surreal and something I can't put in words.

"Mr. Sterling." A deep voice invades the chaos I'm centered in. "Open your eyes."

I have no idea how many times that phrase is repeated before my eyes flit open several times before finally popping open. When light invades, that's when I tumble right into full panic mode. My limbs flail as if a storm has whirled into my world.

"What's going on?" A familiar voice interrupts amidst the anarchy. "Get back. He needs space. Get back."

Blonde, curly hair cascades over me. Bertie. Her familiar gentle smile from days long ago is vacant. She's in full business mode. Oh, wait, that's right— she's a doctor. My surgeon. Her words. My words.

The stale gray ceiling dotted with bright lights the last thing I remember staring at.

"Back off," she barks one more time, leaning over me.

Just the sound of her voice calms my insides. As each second ticks by, my stiffened body melts back into the bed. Bertie's hands roam over my chest, even though she's tugging at shit and pulling the obstacle out of my throat.

My chest jolts forward. Warm palms cup my cheeks. It's the briefest of comfort I need.

"Cody, breathe. Try to stay calm." Bertie's fingers cup my face. "You're just fine. You're just fine."

Her words do soothe the panic, but not enough. My body isn't connected to my soul, and I swear I'm about to grow crazy. It's not until Bertie drops her cheek down close to my ear that I can ignore all the buzzing and chaos surrounding me. The lyrics of "Fast Car" tickle every single one of my senses. It's what I need to ground myself. My heaving chest soothes out into a rhythmic pace, even though the raw and burning sensation in my throat ignites to an all new level.

I open my mouth to ask for water, but when nothing comes out, I manage with all of my energy to grab my throat. I'm only able to weakly wave my hand in a gesture. A strangled grunt comes from somewhere inside me. Bertie picks up on all of it. She shouts out orders, and before I know it, there's something wet touching my lips. It's just enough to dampen the desert also known as the inside of my mouth.

"Stand back, Doctor Cooper," a gruff voice barks.

She doesn't move, applying more moisture to the inside of my mouth. Every time I struggle to swallow, the razor blades inside my throat sharpen. With each action, it's a slicing motion causing my insides to groan and grimace.

"Stand back." The same stern voice reverberates around wherever in the hell I am. "This is your last warning, Doctor Cooper."

She doesn't move, gracefully rolling the swab of sweet, sweet cold liquid around my mouth. She hasn't stopped her perfect whispering of the song lyrics in my ear. Wetness rolls down my cheeks, and I know it's my tears. Bertie begins rocking back and forth. All of her and everything she's doing calms my insides until I gain my bearings.

"Call security, now." That fucking voice invades my calmness once again.

"No!" Bertie jolts up.

The alarm or security system goes off, all sorts of piercing noises throttling my entire being right back into panic.

"Stop," another random voice invades. "He needs her."

"No," the dickhead booms again.

Bertie's hands are right back on me, easing me back into my body. She doesn't move for a long time until she's pried from me. And once she is, Jessie, Jules, and Max are standing by my bed. The look on Jessie's face says it all. She's gone once again. I do my best to glance around the room, finding it damn near impossible to lift my head.

"Relax, man." Jessie covers my shoulder with his hand. "You're good and awake now."

Awake? What the hell? Jessie reads the questions and confusion blanketing my features.

"You went in for your hip surgery. They don't know what in the hell happened, but you flatlined. There's no rhyme or reason. You've been on a ventilator and slipped into a coma. You just came out of it."

"Ber—" I raise my hand, pointing at the door.

Jessie nods. "Yeah, she was your surgeon. Checked on you every day."

I shake my head back and forth, screwing up my eyebrows.

"You've been out two weeks, man."

A new doctor enters the room. Jessie talks to him like they are old friends. I ignore all of it, still confused as hell. The man tries talking to me. I answer his simple questions and do the reflex tests, tugging and pushing on his hands the best I can do.

The overload of information drains my already exhausted body. I can't handle any of it. A nurse enters the room, pumping something into my IV with a needle and syringe.

"You need your rest, Cody. You've been through a lot."

And just like that, my eyelids grow heavy with slumber.

Chapter 8

Cody

"You're getting released today." Britt's bright smile lights up the dim hospital room.

"You seem a bit too excited about that," I respond, tossing my journal to the side.

"Well, you're kind of a grumpy asshole," she whispers, overexaggerating the last word.

Britt was a welcome gift after the Hitler-type nurses in the ICU. I swear I couldn't rip a fart or burp without one of them rushing in. I've lost count of how many days I've been in this shit hole. Recovery has been hell since I should've been up and walking after waking up from the surgery. That didn't happen, and now I genuinely do feel like a ninety year old who lived life damn hard. I'm able to walk but not without someone guarding me as if I was a toddler with wobbly legs under me.

Relying on pain meds to get back up and going or the need for home care for a few weeks isn't something I like to boast about. Guess when you flatline on the operating table, people take that shit serious. The battery of tests they've put me through have been grueling.

There haven't been any other complications since I came to. Jessie and Jules have visited as much as they have been able to and should be on their way to take me home. Bertie has been a ghost. I've seen her in the hall, but she's diverted her gaze at every meeting.

Her message before the surgery is the one thing that's remained crisp and clear in my memory. Everything after that is a blur. I gave up. I was done. And now here I am, irritated and exhausted and ready to go home. I can't wait to get my bar back up and going. Get into the swing of things where my mind will remain busy. I have plans, and I have been jotting them down in my journal. There are plans that are realistic and plans that will never happen, but it does help writing them out, as much as it makes me sound like a pussy.

Britt checks my vitals, grabs the tray of shitty-ass food from the delivery person, and slings it onto my bedside table. Then she pushes my mug of water in front of my face.

"Drink up. Don't want you all constipated again. Because you were meaner than mean." She winks at me.

Before she exits the room, I holler at her, "Thanks for everything, Britt."

"It's my job. Don't go getting a big head." She grips the side of the wall, worrying her bottom lip. "You really should talk to her before you leave."

"Britt," I grit out.

"Fine, asshole." She slaps the wall.

Britt has grown to be a good friend. My first instincts about her were right. She's a good person through and through. She mentioned Bertie once, and I let her talk but then told her to never mention her name again. Turns out the two of them are pretty damn good friends. Bertie overreacted that first day in my room and has since apologized. I could sense Britt wanted to tell me more about the situation, but I didn't allow it.

The phone connected to my room rings, and I know who it is. I give Britt one final wave.

"What do you want?" I growl then smile, knowing going home is a matter of hours away.

"See you're still a little bitch." Jessie's chuckle echoes from the other end.

"I got your bitch," I banter back, glancing out the window at the late snow storm pouring down.

"Bad news." He pauses. "They closed the interstate and no idea when they'll open it again. We are about three hours from ya, and the roads are hell."

Silence streams between us. This has to be a nasty, cruel punchline to the joke from hell.

"Okay," I stutter out.

"Jules is calling the hospital to see if you can stay a bit longer until they open the roads."

"No." I shake my head.

"Yes," he replies.

I hang my head for a moment, the tension in my knuckles building as I grip the phone. "Hell no. I'll check myself out and hole up in a hotel room until this shit passes."

"No, you won't," I hear Jules holler from the other end of the phone.

"Jesus, I'm fine, you guys. You brought my wallet and credit cards back the last time you were here. Shit, they'll have better food than this place. Drive back home and text me when you're there safe."

"No, he can't do that."

Jessie cuts off Jules' momma bear rant. "Call us when you get settled in. Man, I feel like shit about this."

"Nah, don't. Nothing has gone right since…" I don't finish my sentence. Nothing has gone my way since rushing into that fire. If I'm being honest with myself, nothing has happened the way I wanted it for years upon years. "I'll be good and jingle ya in a few hours, man."

"Sounds good." There's a silent pause.

"Don't, Jessie," I warn him. He's been on the damn Bertie train as well.

He clears his throat. "Love ya."

"You too. Talk soon." I hang up the phone, scrubbing the stubble on my face. The clean-shaven, slick manwhore is long gone. I push away the tray of dog food, swing my legs over the bed, feeling the stiffness that has settled in, and reach for my cell phone charging on the counter. I damn near fall off the bed before I grab it.

You'd think Jules was my own damn mom. She packed everything for me on their last visit from my wallet to three clean pairs of boxers. You'd think I was going to shit my pants a couple times on the way home. I didn't give her hell, though, because she also brought home-baked goodies that were gone in a matter of seconds.

I search hotel rooms, not wanting to spend the night at the cockroach throne, and come up with a master plan to fool the discharge nurse. It won't be an easy task, but I'm a determined man. I want more than anything to chill out in a bed in a pair of my boxers, chowing down on greasy delivery pizza.

Once my bags are packed and I've flirted enough with the discharge nurse, she leaves me at the curb of the hospital. The stars must have been aligned for once—she was paged to a code red. The wet snowflakes fall on the tip of my nose, and even though the air is chilled and freezing, it exhilarates every part of me. I relish the freedom for a few beats before pushing myself out of the wheelchair. Didn't need that son of a bitch, but it was hospital policy or some nonsense.

I rest against a pillar, downloading the Uber app because God knows I'm Uber in my parts and don't even get paid for that shit. Once it's downloaded and my payment is connected, I'm about to press the button for "request a ride" when I hear my name.

I turn to see Bertie wiping tears away from her swollen eyes. "What are you doing out here?"

She tugs a hood over her head with most of her features being swallowed up by the huge snowflakes. Her blonde hair I love so much and hunger to run my fingers through is hidden under a purple hood that's now white.

I shrug, not having the energy to lie anymore. "Interstate is closed. Jessie and Jules had to turn back home. Gonna find an Uber to take me to the Best Western."

"Cody."

Then there's peaceful silence floating between us with the sparkle and glitter of the snow surrounding us.

"What?" I glance down, unable to look her in the eye.

"You can't be alone. You know this. A hotel?" The tips of her boots crunch on the snow and come into my vision.

I glance up at her. "Remember, you don't give two shits about me, Bertie. I'm not your problem."

"Cody, not now." She crosses her arms. "You're on strong pain meds and still recovering. You can't be alone."

"I'll order room service. They can check on me," I spit out.

"No. Why didn't you just stay in the hospital until this storm passes?"

"Again, not your worry, Bertie. Or should I call you Roberta?"

"Enough!" she screams, getting up in my face. "I am sorry for what I said to you before the surgery. I am sorry you flatlined under my hands. You have no idea what I've put myself through, Cody."

I'm taken aback by her words. She was so damn adamant that I was nothing but trash in her life. Hell, not even a memory according to her. I remain silent, having nothing to say.

"You have two options right now, Cody." She takes the tiniest of steps back. "You can march your stubborn ass back in that hospital and tell them your circumstances or…" Her determined words die off as she nibbles on her bottom lip. She squares her shoulders and raises her chin high. "Or you can come home with me until Jessie can make it up here."

"Excuse me?" I cough on my words, knowing this has to be some damn hallucination or shit.

"You heard me. I cannot and will not allow you to check yourself into a hotel room. Not gonna happen."

"Stop me." I push off the pillar, walking a few steps and feeling the ache begin in my hip. I shake the snow from my overgrown hair, confused as shit.

"Security," Bertie hollers over her shoulder, catching the attention of a guard who just walked out of the hospital. She cups her hands around her mouth, hollering the word again.

"What the hell are you doing?" I take a long stride toward her. "I'm fine. Go home to your fiancé."

That was a low blow. I can even admit that. I heard the nurses chatter and rattle on about the break-up. They kept it pretty much hush around me, but in the hospital, nothing seems to be a secret.

She turns toward the security guard, not acknowledging my nasty comment. I watch for few seconds before I realize what she's doing. Bertie is marching her ass right over to the security guard.

"Stop," I holler, leaving my bag at my feet and walking as fast as I can, which is slow as shit, especially on the slick sidewalk. The last thing I need to do is fall on my ass.

"Is there a problem?" The towering guard with salt and pepper hair joins the conversation.

"No," I blurt out.

He rests his hand on his hip, near his gun, not believing me. I don't blame him with the look of exasperation on Bertie's face and her swollen eyes.

The entire scene doesn't look good at all.

"Go on." He sounds annoyed.

"My car's battery is dead, and we were just troubleshooting here," I offer, knowing I just signed away my freedom to Bertie.

Bertie darts an eyebrow up. "Yeah, I'm just going to give him a lift. I was going to see if you had jumper cables."

"Well, I don't," he says, taking his hand off his hip and relaxing a tick. "Do you two know each other?"

Bertie nods. "Long-time friends."

I control the snort desperate to escape from me.

"Well, you two travel safe." He goes back to his post under a large awning, avoiding the snowfall. Bertie and I weren't as smart; we were now covered in a thick layer of snow.

We don't exchange any more words as I follow Bertie to her car. I do my best knocking off all the snow before taking my seat, embarrassed how long it takes me to get settled in and buckled up. I glance in the back seat without thinking, spotting the bright yellow booster seat and random stuffed animals. There's so much I don't know about Bertie. She made it damn obvious I don't deserve to, either, and I can't argue.

Bertie grips her steering wheel, staring straight forward. "You never told Jessie the truth about us."

I flop my head back on the headrest, letting out a loud exhale. "No, I didn't."

"Why?" She continues staring forward, showing no emotions.

"Sounds ridiculous now, but I was protecting you.

I never wanted it to get back to you."

She snorts at that. "Bethany made sure I knew."

"I know it doesn't matter, but I've beat myself up over it for years."

"I know," she whispers. "I really wish you would've told me back then. I think it's something we could have worked through. I may have been absorbed in my studies, but I wasn't blind, Cody. I knew how she was."

"Doesn't make it right." I roll my head to study her, but she's clutching her cards in a firm grip, revealing nothing.

"No, it doesn't." She wipes a stray tear from under her eyes and finally glances at me. The pain that is obviously ripping her in half torments me. "Cody, you died. Everything flashed before my eyes. I've never been so scared in my life. If I'm telling the truth, I'm still rattled."

I reach over and grab her hand, giving it a gentle squeeze. "Bertie, it's not your fault. None of it is, and it's killing me you're sitting here beating yourself up over any of this."

She offers me a gentle smile, clutching my hand. "Do you think we can start over?"

I freeze, knocked down with a tornado of shock. A miracle has been placed before me, one that I knew would never happen. I nod then clear my throat. "Yeah, I'd give anything for that."

"No need to give anything." She squeezes her eyes shut. "You're going to think I'm crazy, but I swear the universe is pushing us back into each other's lives. Me being put on your surgery, you nearly dying, and now this storm. I think we better listen to what the higher powers are telling us."

"Thank you, Bertie, thank you so much. I'll be the best houseguest and friend you could ever ask for. No leaving the toilet seat up and I'll always do a courtesy flush."

This gains a giggle from her, lightening the mood. "Always the gentlemen."

"Now can you start the car? Because I'm freezing the family jewels off."

"Cody Sterling, you haven't changed a bit have you?" she asks, turning the key to start her car. Music blares on the highest volume as cold air blasts me in the face.

"Jesus." I turn down the air while Bertie lowers the volume of the radio. I reach over and turn the radio up a bit and wink at her. "Nice song."

We sing every word to "Fast Car" on the short drive to her place.

Chapter 9

Bertie

I manage to give Cody the short tour of my home and get all his stuff settled in before Nell and Cody burst through the door. Everything happened so fast, I didn't have the chance to give either of them a heads up. Nell has never been one for being subtle. I cringe, thinking about the train wreck that's about to go down.

"Mom!" Cody squeals as she flies down the hall. "Second day and I didn't have to flip my card. I ignored everything mean people said. Oh, and at the learning center, I even passed a test and got candy."

Cody rattles on and on. I let her get everything out, praise her, and then scoop her up in my arms. "Hey, I need to tell you and Nell something."

"I'm in the kitchen," Nell hollers. "You don't have shi—crap for food."

Even after years of being around Cody, Nell still catches herself cursing all the time.

I round the corner. "Okay, listen up, girls. We have a house guest."

Nell drops the jar of pickles onto the counter. "You, we, what?"

"Who, Mom?" Cody inquisitively stares at me, running her tiny fingers through my messy hair.

I clear my throat. "My friend was going home today, but the snowstorm closed down the interstate and…"

Cody, the sinfully sexy man, rounds the corner at the same exact moment. Nell's mouth falls open, and Cody wiggles in my arm.

"Hey." She points at him. "I know you. You stole my name."

Cody smirks, limping into the room. He's doing really well as far as his recovery but still has lots of PT to get through.

"You got me." He raises his hands in surrender.

"Come meet my dog!" Cody wiggles out of my arms, racing towards the yapping, high-pitched barks from Scotty.

Cody follows like a diligent little soldier. I make a mental note to talk to her about letting Cody rest.

"What the hell is going on?" Nell hisses.

I lean a hip on the counter, crossing my arms, ready for this battle. "He was going to stay in a hotel until the interstate opened back up. He can't be by himself. He needs care."

"Okay." She overexaggerates the word, urging me to go on.

"So I invited him here." I shrug. "Actually forced him here. It's the least I can do."

"You don't owe him anything, Bertie. I have no

idea why you have that messed-up idea bottled up in you. No freaking idea."

"I don't owe him anything, but I want him here, Nell. I'm sorry if you don't understand that. He needs help. Yes, we have a past, but I damn well know he'd do the same for me if I was in the same situation."

"And exactly how are you going to help him when you work minimum…" she drags out the last word, "…forty hours a week?"

"I have that figured out."

She shakes her head, still reeling in shock. "Be careful."

I'm grateful she's too focused on lecturing me and doesn't ask about my plan.

"I lost my best friend for nearly a year last time he was in your life, Bertie. You were so hurt and curled up in yourself. You can't do that this time. You have a daughter."

"Nell." Her name comes out in a warning tone. "If you think I'd ever do anything to put my daughter at risk, then I think you need to leave."

"Stop." She walks over to me, wrapping me up in a hug. "It came out wrong. I'm an ass. I should've said just don't get hurt again."

"I won't," I whisper.

Cody sprints back into the kitchen, ripping open the pantry door, digging around for Scotty's favorite dog treat. The evil little pooch is right on her tail. Moments later, Cody joins us.

"Nell." He nods. "Long time. Nice seeing ya."

She purses her lips together. I pinch the back of her arm, warning her to play nice. "Yeah, you too, Cody."

"What?" Cody wipes her curls from her face, looking at Nell.

"Dear Lord, we are going to need nicknames for you two," I say.

"Nope." Cody places her hands on her hips, shaking her head. "Not for me. He stoleded my name."

We all erupt in laughter. Only if she knew the story behind it. One day she will when she's old enough to understand the meaning of true love.

"I'm fine with a nickname, but not sure if any my current ones are appropriate, though." Cody pulls the chair out from the dining room table, settling in.

"What are they?" Scotty steals the treat from Cody's hand.

I watch the big bad Cody Sterling grow pale and at a loss for words. It's a rare sight and a damn adorable one.

"Douche canoe," Nell mutters low enough only I hear her.

I walk over to the table, deciding to save Cody from the start of this awkward conversation. "How about we call Cody..." I place a palm on his shoulder.

My Cody jumps in before I get the chance to finish my sentence, and quite honestly, I had nothing. Absolutely nothing.

"I remain Cody." She pats her chest. "Since you stoleded my name, you become Junior."

Cody, or shall I say Junior, mulls over the idea, tilting his head, acting as if he's in deep thought. "Sounds like a plan, Stan."

"Perfect." Cody claps. "What's for dinner,

Mom?"

"I'm going to order pizza and salad from your favorite place."

"Yes." She fist pumps the air. "Nell, you staying?"

"Naw, squirtanator. I've had a long day. I'll see you on Friday when I pick you up for dance."

The two of them exchange hugs, kisses, and then top it off with their secret handshake. It's a ridiculous ritual the two do every time they part. I follow Nell out, leaving the two Codys at the dining room table, deep in conversation about pizza toppings. Just from the first few suggestions exchanged, I can tell they'll never see eye to eye.

"Love you, Nell." I wrap my arms around her and squeeze the crap out of her. "You'll always be my person."

"I love you, too." She pinches my ass, causing me to jump and squeal then rub out the pain.

"So, something else happened today." I pause, wriggling my lips back and forth. If she blew up over Cody staying here, then she's going to lose her ever-loving shit with the next news. "You know I was taken off surgeries for a while. But what I didn't tell you is that I was written up for my actions when Cody woke up in ICU. I was told to stand down and never did. Garrett took it to the hospital board, and they put me on paid leave today until they decide what to do."

"What?" she screeches. "What in the hell? Why did they wait so long and can they do that?"

I nod, answering every single one of her questions. I wrap my arms around my middle, warding off the bitter cold. "I have no idea why they waited so long, but I could guess it's Garrett's doing. He warned me I'd regret leaving him, and I guess he came through."

"He can't pull that bullshit."

"Well, he is my supervisor and has every right to report incidents for review."

"God, I hate him. Junior," a full megawatt grin appears on her face when she uses Cody's nickname, "is looking better and better all the time."

"We are just friends. Nothing else."

"Yeah, keep telling yourself that." Nell slaps my ass and trots to her car, doing a few whirls in the middle of the snowfall.

The girl loves the snow. She'll be on the mountainside for days enjoying the snow. She's a ski bum who lives for the season. I never understood it since she's so girly, but the woman shreds the snow or whatever you call it. She's been teaching Cody while I stay in the lodge, cuddled up with a good book and coffee.

I shut the front door and lock it out of habit. A thunderous yell comes from the kitchen, followed by shouting.

"Son of a bitch."

I race into the kitchen to find Cody whipping his leg in the air with Scotty dangling from his big toe. He has his teeth sunk in, with no signs of giving up anytime soon.

"No. No." Cody jumps up and down, trying to grab Scotty. When she does get hold of him and tugs, Scotty doesn't budge, only sinking his little fangs deeper into Cody's flesh.

Cody continues to cuss and groan in pain. I'm able to reach into the chaos, grab Scotty by his middle, and pry the jaws of life from Cody's toes. Once he's released, blood soaks through Cody's sock.

"Mom." Cody's chin quivers as she points at the mess. "Mom."

She grows panicked. My little rough and tough tomboy doesn't handle blood well at all. There will be no way in hell she follows in my footsteps.

"Baby, go get me a damp rag, the ouch medicine, and a Band-Aid."

She nods, tears welling up in her eyes.

"Naw, you don't have to. It's not that bad."

"Yes, it is, Junior."

"I'm going," Cody offers before darting out of the room.

I kneel, tugging off his sock. "So I, uh, should've warned you about Satan, also known as Scotty, demon dog from hell."

"That would've been helpful." Cody winces when I give the sock a final tug, pulling it from his foot. "He's a little prick. The bastard attacked me out of nowhere. I wasn't even moving my feet or playing with him."

I reach up, ripping a paper towel from the top of the island. "Yeah, so he's very protective of Cody. I can't tell you how many times the little ass has nipped at me."

"Are you serious?" His eyebrows shoot up in surprise.

"Dead serious." I begin dabbing around the bite to see what I'm dealing with. "Two weeks in and I nearly took him back to the pound, but Cody was already in love with him. Those two do everything together. So my guess is Scotty was jealous Cody was paying attention to you."

A warm fingertip grazes under my chin, urging me to look up at him. "Why did you name her Cody?"

My fingertips hover over the wound. I don't look away or flinch at his question. It's time the truth comes out. Cody's dad didn't even know. He thought I was crazy for giving our girl a boy name, but he was a gentleman and let me name her.

"Because I love you and always have and knew the only other thing I could ever love as much as you would be my own daughter."

He cups my cheek, brushing his thumb along my jawline. "Thank you for telling me."

That was easy. He doesn't pry for more information or make the situation uncomfortable.

"Here, Mom." Cody shoves the items in my face then turns to Scotty, who followed her up to her room. "Bad boy! You're getting a whipping."

Cody shakes her pointer finger at her dog. Scotty's large ears droop down, and he tucks his tail between his legs.

Junior whispers, "Will he bite her?"

I shake my head no, knowing what will come next. She scoops the dog up in her arms, squeezes her eyes shut, bringing her hand up in a spanking motion, but when it comes down, she pats Scotty on the bum. It's nowhere near a spanking. Hell, it probably feels good to the pooch. Junior stifles down a laugh.

"You don't bite Junior again or you'll get another whipping. Do you hear me, Scotty?" She tucks her best friend under her arm and trots up to her room.

"Now that's the funniest shit I've ever seen." Junior shakes his head.

"See, now you can understand why I can never get rid of that little bastard." I finish cleaning up the blood around the bite. I decide not to tell him I'm putting peroxide on it and just do it quick. There's only a slight jump, and before you know it, he's bandaged up.

I brush my hands off in a job well done before popping up and washing them. "So, what kind of pizza do you like?"

He quirks an eyebrow at me.

"Fine." I shake my head. "Do you still favor Canadian bacon, pineapple, and jalapeno?"

"Nailed it." He relaxes back a grimace expression on his face. "But I can eat cheese pizza with extra cheese."

Drying my hands, I smile. Of course, he's already willing to give into Cody like he did for me so many years ago. The poor man memorized the periodic table when I was obsessed with it instead of going to movies and the normal things teens do.

"I got you covered." I wink at him. "Hey, are your pills in your bag upstairs?"

He nods.

"Okay, I'll grab them while I'm ordering the pizza."

"It's fine."

But I have the phone to my ear and am jogging up the stairs before he can move. I pass Cody on the way up. She's heading down with a basket full of toys with Scotty right in the middle. With a quick glance,

I can see Junior is about to be introduced to the world of coloring and sticker books.

He has one bag, making it easy to find all of his pills. I glance at each label, making sure he was sent home with all of them. Even after being kicked out of his ICU room, I kept tabs on him through Trent. The bag tumbles to the ground when I whirl around to leave. His wallet tumbles out, laying wide open, causing a picture to free itself. My breathing hitches when I see the candid shot he took of me one day when I was studying. I knew he carried it back then, but by the state of it now, it's clear as day he's never taken it out of his wallet.

In a rush, not wanting to think what that gesture means, I stuff everything back in the bag and place it on the bed. My legs move in a rush down the stairs.

"You can use any color you want, but not yellow, okay?"

"Why is that?" Junior asks, craning his neck to make eye contact with my daughter.

"Because it's my favorite and only one yellow comes in every pack and I don't want you wasting it."

"Cody," I scold her when I walk in. "You have plenty of yellow markers. You can share."

"Naw, it's all right. My favorite color is brown." He snags the fat brown marker.

"Eewww, that's the grossest color ever, Junior."

"Not to me." He shrugs, beginning to shade in the petals of a daisy.

"You are so weird." Cody shakes her head, causing her rat's nest of hair to shake everywhere.

I grab a bottle of water and count out the pills

Junior needs to take, holding back the one he needs to take with food, mentally berating myself for being so damn doctory. I can't help it.

"Here you go." I slide the pills and bottle of water on the table. "I'll get the one you need to take with food after dinner."

"Thanks, Doc." He winks up at me. "But you seriously don't have to worry about any of this. I got it."

"Okay." I play with the hem of my shirt. "You've already done enough."

Junior picks up his cellphone, typing out a quick text then pulling up another browser window. *It's none of my business,* I repeat over and over in my head. I can't even imagine the amount of texts he has waiting on him. Friends…that's what we are, and it's none of my concern. It seems the determined monster called jealousy seated deep down in my gut doesn't seem to care.

"Hey, what's your address?" He looks up from his phone.

I twirl a lock of my hair, tilting my head. "Why?"

"Jules. She's so damn protective, wants to know."

"Oh." I fire off the address, finishing right when the doorbell chimes.

Junior stands faster than I thought possible and makes it to the door before me. In all fairness, I could've shoved him and beat him but didn't think it was the best choice. He opens the door and produces a card from his back pocket before I even have the chance to argue with him.

I clear my throat once the door shuts again. I'm stuck holding three boxes full of pizza and salad.

"Cody," I warn.

"I'm not about to stay at your house, have you pay for my food and fetch my pills. Some things don't change, Bertie, and one of them is me taking care of you."

"Thank you."

He follows me back into the kitchen, not so fast this time. "Just glad I tucked it in my pocket. I had it ready to check into a hotel room. Didn't get a chance to grab my wallet from the bag when Nurse Ratchet swooped into my room."

I laugh out loud. "Let me guess. You're referring to Cheryl."

"Yep, that woman scares the shit out of me."

"You can't say shit, Junior. It's a bad word." Cody points her yellow marker at him.

He actually blushes in embarrassment. "I'm so sorry. I'll clean up my mouth."

We settle in at the table, eating right from the boxes. I consider myself lucky since the other two both despise salad. I enjoy the whole thing, inhaling it. Natural conversation ensues as we chow down. It's as if we've been doing this for years. Nothing is forced. It blows my mind when I think about it. Garrett never once sat at this table with us. He always claimed to be too busy. All excuses. It's just another reminder I did the right thing.

Chapter 10

Cody

A full night's sleep does a man good. Crisp clean sheets, an unsupervised hot shower, and overhearing Bertie tuck in her little Miss Cody, I feel complete. Can't explain it away and end up having more questions than before. I listen to the two of them talk to a picture of Cody's dad and am left wondering.

The day's events drained me, leaving me no energy to stay up late into the night thinking everything through. As soon as my body landed on the mattress, I was out. Woke up to a note by my bedside, telling me that she ran Cody to school and will be back soon. A bottle of water and my morning pills is right next to it.

I shake my head at Bertie's thoughtfulness. The woman's heart is the biggest I've ever seen or come across. She's something else. I down the pills then decide on another hot shower.

When I make it down to the living room, Bertie is

perched on the couch with her legs crossed, messy bun perched on top of her head while she studies her computer screen. She nibbles on her bottom lip and twists her nose. There's no denying something or someone is stressing her out.

I clear my throat, not wanting to scare the shit out of her.

"Oh, hey." Her head pops up. "Sleep well?"

"Like a damn baby," I reply.

"I left a bagel, cream cheese, and some fruit out for you." Her attention goes back to the computer screen.

"Thanks, Bertie." I don't tell her that Jules packed me my favorite protein shakes and I already downed one. I clean up the food she left for me, deciding an apple sounds good. The inside of her house makes me smile—it's simple, not extravagant. It's perfection. Cody's drawings and goofy photographs of the two of them are plastered to the front of the refrigerator by colorful magnets. Most of them are yellow.

Speaking of yellow, the doorbell rings. I'm pretty sure I know what's waiting on the other side.

"I'll grab it," I holler.

Of course, Bertie ignores my comment, meeting me at the door.

A tall, skinny, nerdy boy stands there with bags full of groceries. "Delivery for a Cody Sterling."

"That's me." I open the door wider, helping the young kid carry the bags in.

"Thank you." I nod, feeling all sort of weird. I've never done this before. Am I supposed to tip these home delivery people? God knows the tiny town I live in has nothing like this. Not even close.

"Have a nice day and thank you for using our service." He bops down the steps, practically skipping to his car.

"What is this?" Bertie asks, eyeing all the bags.

"Well," I run my hand through my still damp hair, "I went online last night with the intentions of ordering Cody a pack of yellow markers. Came across this home delivery place and figured I could help out with groceries."

She reaches into one of the bags, pulling out a jar of spicy nacho cheese, then snags the bag of Puffy Cheetos. "Yet another thing that hasn't changed over the years."

"Give me that, you thief." I reach out for the bag, but Bertie is quicker, holding the bag over her head while racing back to her spot on the couch.

"Oh, don't you dare." I take the seat next to her, not missing the fact she snaps the lid to her laptop shut before I can see what was on the screen.

My junk food bone is hankering hard for a binge. I sure as shit haven't had any in a long time. Bertie struggles, twisting the lid off the top of the jar of nacho cheese.

"Give it here, weak sauce." I grab it from her when she protests. "I thought your hands were skilled."

Bertie winces.

"Shit, too soon. I wasn't thinking." The lid pops from the jar, and sharp cheese scent fills the air.

Bertie bends forward, and I swear to God if she bursts into tears, I have no idea what I'll do. What happens next is the last thing I expected to hear. She

91

erupts into a fit of maniacal laughter. She doesn't stop until she's wiping tears away from her eyes.

"You should've seen your face when you realized what you said." Now she's clutching her stomach.

I bump her shoulder with mine and mumble around a mouth full of Cheetos, "Asshole. Not funny."

We sit in silence for a long time, dipping our Cheetos and crunching them down.

"Do you think this is weird?"

"What?" I ask, licking my fingers.

"Us. This," she responds.

"First off, this," I point to our mid-morning snack, "can never be considered weird. It's the food of the gods."

"Idiot." She smacks my shoulder. "I'm talking about us. Do you think it's weird?"

I shrug. "Not weird, but maybe a bit odd and surreal."

"I agree." She nods, popping a Cheeto in her mouth. "I think I'm done trying to figure out why it feels so natural, even after what we've been through and all the years that have passed."

"I get that," I agree. "I can't explain it, either. Honestly, never thought you'd look at me again. Still find it hard to believe. The only thing I can think of is that it is our time. Maybe we had to experience a little bit of life before our circle connected again."

"I'm scared," she whispers.

"Of?" I prompt her.

"A permanently broken circle that can't be mended."

"Me too," I whisper. "I do know one thing for

certain. I'll fight like hell before that ever happens."

"You will?" She lays her head on my shoulder.

"Only thing worth living for."

"Don't say that."

"It's the truth, Bertie."

We remain silent for a long time before she's the first to break the silence.

"Tell me everything, Cody. I want to know it all."

She feels me tense next to her, and she's quick to correct herself.

"Tell me about the years I missed with you."

I slouch back on the couch, resting my head and wiggling just a bit to move my hip. When I sit still too long, it stiffens up something fierce. I tell her everything, about buying the old garage and turning it into a bar and how I've remained close to Jessie through the years. Then I proceed to explain Jessie's family dynamics.

"So Max found out he had a kid he never knew about?" she asks, letting her arm rest across my abdomen.

"Yeah, it was crazy as hell. He moved into an old farmhouse behind the bar since it was closer to where his son lived. It was ugly as hell. His son, Finn, was in foster care, and it was actually his teacher who contacted Max. The rest is sort of history."

She lifts her head to stare at me. "Sorta? Go on, tough guy."

She smooths her fingertips in lazy circles on the top of my shirt. With the combination of her coconut lime scent, her perfect body pressed against mine, things down south start to stir to life. I do my best to ignore it.

"Long story straight."

Bertie cuts me off with her loud bout of laughter. "Long story short, Cody. I still remember the day in high school when you said that, and you were seriously thinking that's how the saying went."

"Yeah, and I promised you that day it made sense and I was sticking with it the rest of my life."

"You know that's the thing I've always loved about you. You've never let anyone change who you are."

I force myself to shove her sentiment of love to the side. It's a glimmer of hope, and knowing me, I'll steal that and run with it. I'll push this way too fast and ruin my second chance. Never believed in them, but now there's nothing else I want in this world.

"Anyway, long story straight. Finn's mom was batshit crazy, all hyped on drugs. She and her junkie boyfriend broke into Kate's house and beat her and set the place ablaze. I was called first since I live the closest and was a volunteer firefighter. I didn't think and rushed in, knowing Kate was in there. I found her near the back door, and just as I got to her, one of the center beams from the ceiling fell and landed on me. I had just enough time to dive on top of her to protect her. And now, truly, the rest is history."

"Holy shit. That's where you got the burns from."

"Yeah." I roll my head, sniffing her hair then letting my lips run along the top of her head for the briefest of seconds. "And my busted-to-hell hip."

"And let me guess, you despise being called a hero even though you are one."

"Bingo." I squeeze her closer to me. "Now your turn. Tell me everything."

94

"Well." She sits up, wiggles around, until she's sitting cross-legged on the couch facing me. I instantly miss her body pressed against mine but also relish in the fact she wants to face me as she shares a piece of herself with me. "It's not as fascinating as yours. I made it through college, got into medical school, and was on top of life."

She fiddles with her fingers, averting her gaze.

"Go on."

"It's awkward," she admits.

I cover her hands, squeezing them gently, urging her to go on. "No, it's not. I want to know."

"I met a guy. He was the first one I really dated since you. There had been casual dates but no one who held my attention. Bradley and I had a lot in common, mainly our drive to succeed. Before we knew it, our study sessions turned heated. It was comfortable. I loved him but didn't love, love him if that makes sense?"

"It does," I respond.

"It's ironic that two med students ignored the lesson about the birds and the bees. I got pregnant. I was, of course, devastated for a few weeks. It was Bradley who held my hand and told me we'd get through it. It wasn't in either of our plans, but we did it. When Cody was ten months old, Bradley was struck on the interstate by a drunk driver and died on impact."

"I am so sorry, baby." I lean forward, placing a kiss on her cheek, wiping away the stray tears with the pads of my thumbs, and then tug her into my lap as she begins to tear up.

"Nell put everything on hold so I could get

through med school. I was so close but so far away. She moved here with us when I got my internship, and we've never left." Bertie settles deeper into my lap. "The hardest thing is watching Cody grow up without her father. It hurts my heart every time she asks questions about him. I want her to know everything about him. It just reminds me how much I miss him. He was my best friend for years."

That comment should hurt, but it doesn't. Bradley sounds like a damn good guy who took care of her. Hell, he gave her Cody, my namesake, and I could never disrespect or hold anger toward him for that.

"Thank you." I kiss the top of her head. "You're one hell of a woman, stronger than I could ever be. You're the true hero here."

She snorts. "Hardly. Then there's Garrett. There hasn't been another man since Bradley. I just didn't have any spare time. Garrett swooped in and wooed me right into being an idiot. Nell and Trent, your doctor, never were fans of him. I ignored their warnings. He became possessive, pushing a future on me. The engagement was a joke and done in public so everyone thought him the hero. The breaking point was when he offered me no support as my boss or boyfriend after your surgery. I gave him back the ring and have never felt better about a decision that I made."

"I'm sorry. You shouldn't have been put in that position, and I should've requested another surgeon, but I was being selfish."

"It never should've happened. The real kicker was Garrett couldn't stand Cody. He never wanted to be around her or take her with us. I separated the two worlds, and that wasn't fair."

"Hell no, it's not, and now I really hate the cocksucker."

She lets out a loud sigh. I can tell there's more she's not telling me, but I don't push her.

Chapter 11

Bertie

"I let her ride the bus home two days a week when I know I'll be here. She loves it." I bend down, plucking a weed growing next to my mailbox.

"I miss her energy when she's at school." Cody tugs his hoodie down tighter on his head. The snow hasn't shown any signs of stopping over the last four days. I'm not one to complain, but I don't even want to think about what's going to happen when it's time for him to go. It's going to crush me.

"What the hell am I, chopped liver now?" I shove his shoulder.

"Jealous?" He cocks an eyebrow.

I snort. "Not hardly."

I notice Cody shifting his weight from leg to leg. I've been doing physical therapy with him at home since the roads are so shitty and the PT he'll be seeing on a regular basis is hours away in his hometown. Not only was Cody's hip destroyed in the

98

fire, but one of his shoulders also has limited mobility from an injury he never followed up on. Kicking his ass during PT time is actually quite entertaining and one of my favorite things to do.

"You've been home since I got here, so is it the momma bear in you that hasn't let her ride the bus home until now?" Cody sticks his tongue out, catching a few large snowflakes.

"You're a damn goof." I shake my head. It's the thing I love most about him. "Yes, as you've probably picked up, Cody really struggles in school. I have no idea how to relate to it since I never did."

"Here it comes." Cody bounces up and down on the balls of his feet.

The big yellow bus stops in front of us. It takes several minutes before the door opens and little Cody climbs down the steps with her head down and arms crossed. The bus driver waves me to the door.

"Baby girl, are you okay?" I ask, bending down as she nears us.

When she looks up, her face is tear-streaked and eyes swollen. She doesn't say a word, marching right past us.

"Go." Junior nods at the bus driver continuing to wave me over. "I'll go inside with her."

The gruff bus driver barks at me. "Are you her mother?"

"Yes, I am." I square my shoulders.

"She's no longer allowed on the bus. She picked a fight with Belle and punched her in the nose. I've got blood everywhere."

"Um, how do you know Cody picked it?"

The bus driver steps back up to the top step and

rolls her eyes. "All the kids said that's what she always does."

Then doors slam shut in my face.

"Bitch," I mutter and manage to keep my middle finger down by my side.

Walking back into the house, my frustration with school and Cody reaches an all-new high. I know she's not a perfect kid. I'm not the blind parent who thinks their child is perfect. But I also don't believe she's always the one who starts everything. This is becoming straight-up bullshit.

I trudge up the steps, doing my best to tamp down my anger. I know it will do no good in this situation. I freeze a few feet before reaching the door to Cody's room. I creep forward, staring through the cracked door. Their voices are clear as day.

"I'm dumb, Junior." Cody slaps down a piece of paper between them on the bed. "I'm the only kid who has to leave the room to go to a special class. My letters are always backwards, and I don't even know them."

"What is this?" he asks, picking up the crumpled paper.

"The story I wrote today." She swipes her arm under her nose. I cringe, hating when she does that. "There's another new kid in our class today. She sat by me on the bus, and I was reading her my story. Belle started making fun of me by telling everyone I'm dumb and don't even know the alphabet. She wouldn't shut up."

"Little bitch," a deep voice mutters.

My sweet little girl slaps her hand over her mouth as her eyes grow wide.

"Shit." Cody runs his hand over his hair, leaving it standing on end. "I suck at this."

"You're funny, Junior." She turns on her bed, sitting cross-legged with a quizzical look plastered on her face. "Do you think I should call her a bitch instead of hitting her?"

"No!" Cody damn near shouts. "No, don't do that. I will quit using those words, and I never want you to use them."

"Then what do I do? She won't quit picking on me until I get so, so mad."

Cody grabs her by the waist, scooting both of them back until they are resting against the headboard with both of their legs stretched out wide. I guarantee the action was so Cody was in a comfortable spot.

"You know, this is a real pickle because even when you grow up, you'll encounter ass—"

"Junior!" Cody giggles. "And what does encounter mean?"

"It means meet. You'll have to work with Belles all the time, and you can't hit them."

"So I just have to be dumb the rest of my life?"

"First of all, we are making a promise right now." He holds out his pinky finger. She follows suit. They connect, and what he says next floods my entire being. "You are never allowed to use the word dumb or stupid. Do you hear me?"

She nods.

"You are not dumb, Cody. Yeah, you may learn differently than others, but you are not dumb, and I never want to hear you say that again."

"Okay."

Scotty takes this moment to trot into the room. I take a step back so I'm not spotted. A vicious growl flows out into the hall, and when I take my position back, I see Scotty growling at Cody before settling into his best friend's lap.

"Richard Noggin," Cody sneers.

"What does that mean?"

I wonder the same thing as my daughter, having no clue what in the hell it means.

"And what does pecker mean? I heard you call Scotty that when he stole your undies out of the bathroom last night."

"Dude, do you hear everything?" Cody shakes his head.

"You yelled it, Junior. Of course, I heard it."

"Another pinky promise." They clasp fingers. "Never tell your mom you heard, and never repeat words you don't know that come out of my mouth."

"Okay."

"I have to tell you something, sweetie. It's not easy to talk about. When I was growing up, I sucked at school. I hated it and struggled the most with reading, so I became a jokester. You know, the class clown?"

Cody nods while cuddling Scotty to her chest. The little attention whore of a dog curls in a ball, relishing each pet.

"Since I wasn't good at school and was embarrassed of it, I made jokes all the time so nobody would know that I was struggling. It wasn't until I was in high school when somebody noticed. She was a good friend of mine and helped me get through school. She let me know it was all right that

102

I learned a different way and helped me with certain tricks so that I could memorize things for a test. My point is that you need to own the way you learn and who you are."

"My mom says the same thing all the time." Cody rolls her eyes.

"Your mom is the person who helped me learn, and I'm thankful for it every day. But I'm going to tell you how you're going to deal with Belle. There will be no more hitting. But I will let you in on some tricks, and I guarantee she and the other mean girls will leave you alone." He winks at my girl. She's completely enraptured, soaking up each one of his words. "People like Belle love the attention when you hit her because she looks like the victim, so everyone's like, 'Oh, Belle, are you okay? Oh, poor, poor Belle.'" He playfully punches the blankets. "We are not giving Belle any more 'ohs.' We are going to show her who is boss."

Cody perks up with this idea. Laying Scotty in her lap, she's all attention and ready for the details. I find that I have tears brimming in my eyes from the scene before me. Nell has always been here for me and Cody, but it's different having a man in my daughter's life. She looks at him differently, and I can tell she listens to him, craving his attention and advice. She respects what he is saying and is eager to do and is eager to learn. I am a bit skeptical about what's going to come next for this man in our life once the snow storm passes. I force myself to remain planted and let them have their time.

"So this little Belle pretty much runs the school right now, correct?"

Cody nods.

"Well, here's the thing: you don't work for anyone. You're the boss of your life and not her bi—" He clears his throat. "You're not her minion." My heart flutters in my chest when a proud smile covers his face. I know beyond a shadow of a doubt he's mentally patting himself on the back.

"When she says mean things to you, you are going to have to ignore her. This will be the hardest thing you'll ever do."

"That's it?" Cody throws her arms up in the air, causing Scotty to dance around in her lap. "That will never work. I don't know how to ignore her. She makes me so, so mad."

Cody raises a finger, shushing her. "That's step one in your plan. You ignore her. The more times you can ignore her, the more pissed off she will grow. She will become madder than you've ever been. So what if she calls you dumb? Who the he—I mean, heck is she to you? She means nothing. Belle wants a reaction out of you. She is going to get so upset that she will resort to meaner things. And once that happens, there are a few little tricks I'm going to teach you."

My little wild child sits up with her full attention now focused on Cody. "Say she's walking past your desk and suddenly you get a cramp in your leg, one that is so bad you feel it in your spine and want to scream out loud."

"Okay," she says, bobbing her head. "But I've never had one."

"Well, trust me, kid, they hurt like h-e-double hockey sticks. And when you do get one, your first reaction will be to stretch out your leg as far as you can. Oops, Belle trips over your foot. Complete accident. You weren't mad, so you can't get in trouble for it." Another wink from Cody. "Accidents do happen. Or say you're in line to go to lunch. And you have to use the restroom, but you don't want to miss lunch, so you start doing the little thing they call the pee-pee dance, swinging your lunchbox around, and oops, your lunchbox gets tangled in her hair. You freak out and try to yank it free. See, you're not mad or even a tad bit upset. There's nothing mean about what happened; it's just one of those pesky accidents. You don't get in trouble, and Belle doesn't ruin your day. Bam, magic!"

"You're so smart, Junior." Cody scoops up Scotty and hugs him to her chest.

He taps his head. "Gotta use this, kid. No more outbursts. Got it?"

"I'm going to try so, so hard." Scotty falls from her arms as she drops him. She hops up to her feet, wrapping her arms around his neck. He remains stock still. "You're my favorite friend, Cody." Louds giggles erupt from her. "Oops, I mean Junior."

"See you already got it down pat, kid." He attempts to ruffle her hair in his best gesture of returning a hug. "You get out those new yellow markers and color for a bit, okay?"

"I can't, Junior. When I get in trouble at school, I'm in big, double deep trouble at home. Mom's face gets red, and she almost cries then tells me no toys, only Scotty."

Junior places a finger over his mouth. "I'll go distract your mom. You take a few minutes to relax and color, okay?"

Cody does her best version of winking at him. As the man who stole my heart so many years ago and never gave it back goes to scoot off the bed, I can tell he's stiff as he moves slow and more than likely in pain, even though he'll never admit it.

I'm snapped from mentally berating myself that he wasn't able to get up and move sooner when in slow motion, Scotty hikes his leg up to take a piss right on Junior's leg. Blonde curls spring toward Scotty, startling the shit out of him while she scoops him up in her tiny arms, but not before he tinkles a bit on Junior's pant leg.

"I swear, Richard Noggin, I'm going to cut off your Richard one day, and we'll see how you like that." The veins in Junior's neck flare to life.

Cody ignores the rant, bouncing over to her desk, setting up her coloring page and an array of yellow markers. I take a few steps back, acting as if I was just bouncing up the stairs. Cody studies the small pee spot on his pants as he walks out with disgust covering his face.

"Really?" I prop a hand on my hip.

"What?" He walks toward me.

"Pecker, calling a child a bitch in front of another child, teaching her to be sneaky on how she gets revenge, shall I go on?" I can't help the smile that creeps on my face. It wasn't the most appropriate talk, but heartwarming and hilarious. The fact alone he put genuine effort and concern into helping my daughter is nothing but a gold medal in my book.

"Are you pissed?"

"Amused and a bit concerned for your mental

stability, but not pissed." I pat his chest, making sure to stay far away from his pant leg. I bite down on my bottom lip. "Just say what's on your mind, Cody. I can tell it's a doozy."

"I want to go over to Belle's house and beat her ass myself, show her what's up."

"Okay, I regret having you tell me. You cannot, and I repeat cannot, talk about kicking a child's ass."

"Shit, I wouldn't. Might pay an older kid to do it, though. There's no damn reason to be so cruel, not to mention Cody is a damn sweet kid."

"You cannot pay kids to beat up another, and also, mister, I'll let it slide tonight, but you can't give in to her when she's in trouble. Somehow and some way she needs to figure out how to react. I've tried everything to instill coping skills, and nothing seems to work. I'm so lost."

He drops his forehead to mine. "I feel for her. I get it. I was a shit reader, and man, that insecurity can eat you whole. My parents could care less. They were only worried about me keeping up with their last name, and I did try my best, but it wasn't up to their standards."

I swallow down the heartache. I never would've thought having a child with a learning disability would be so soul-crushing. Watching your own flesh and blood struggle day in and day out isn't easy. I've never dared complain about it to anyone when children are battling cancer and other life-threatening diseases every single day.

"She was diagnosed with dyslexia a month ago."

"Damn, I'm sorry. Do her teachers help her?"

"The school is good. However, I'm thinking some

of the students are running the classroom, and I'll be visiting the principal about this."

Cody shares Max's son also has a disability and is about the same age as my Cody. My stomach takes it upon itself to growl. The serious moment interrupted.

"You're hungry." He smirks.

"You smell like piss," I spout back at him.

"We're quite the pair, Bertie Cooper."

I pat his chest and step back. "Go change and I'll get the pot roast out of the crockpot."

"Deal."

I watch as Cody struts to his room, admiring his fine backside and broad shoulders, the same skin I used to roam hands over and embrace for hours.

"Hey," I say as he's about to turn into his room. "What does Richard Noggin mean?"

"Hell, you're as bad as her hearing everything. You two have the hearing of a damn bat." He rests his good shoulder on the wall, crossing his arms over his chest, pulling his t-shirt tight. "Put it together, Bertie. What's another name for Richard?"

It takes me a second to put it together. "Dick."

I blush at the mention of the body part and nickname for Richard and repeat it again out loud. "Dick noggin? I don't get it."

He taps his temple. "Noggin. Boy, you have book smarts, but I sure do worry about your street cred, babe."

I watch him tapping the side of his head, and the puzzle pieces fall together. Dickhead. My eyes grow wide at the realization. "You're a Richard Noggin. Go change."

Chapter 12

Cody (AKA Junior)

"Looks like the storm is letting up."

I flop back down on the bed, letting out a breath, frustrated at the news. It's been two days since I gave Cody advice on handling the mean girls at school. I'm pretty sure she hasn't used any of the tactics, but she has also avoided getting into any more scuffles.

"Still snowing like hell here," I reply, and it's the truth. I'm still shocked school hasn't been canceled. All it would take is a stiff wind to cause drifting, and I have no doubt it would be closed.

"Yeah, the roads won't be very good, but the interstate is open," Jessie replies. "Max and I are thinking about heading up tomorrow around three."

I close my eyes and punch the mattress. I could play this several ways, but I'm tired of putting on a façade, the greatest one I've done since I realized I wasn't like the other kids at school. I perfected that act, then when I screwed up with Bertie, I developed the mask to perfection, showing the world I was just fine. But I won't be okay being ripped away from these two girls. In reality, it will crush my damn soul.

"Hey," I rest a palm on my forehead, "I need more time. Really don't want to answer any questions about it."

There's silence on his end. "Are you sure, man?"

"Yeah, never been more certain about anything."

"The interstate is open, but the roads are pretty damn bad," he repeats.

"Yeah." I smile at the ceiling. "The roads are open, but the travels are damn treacherous."

It's a pretty damn accurate description of my current situation.

"You're all-in."

I'm sure it's supposed to be more of a statement than a question.

"I'm all-in. Never believed in it until I was in her presence. I will fight for this with all I have."

"I'll check in with you in a couple of days. Follow your heart, but guard it too, man. She has a life there, and your livelihood is here, five hours away."

"Roger," I reply, hitting the end button on my phone.

The house creeps in an eerie silence. It's the first day that Bertie has had to go back to work. She was very clear in the fact she'd only be gone for six hours and that everything was laid out for me. Hell, I can manage to take my own pills, wipe my ass, and make my way down the stairs to the living area, but I've let her play the doctor role. In true Bertie fashion, she laid everything out except for the goddamn Life Alert bracelet before rushing to take Cody to school.

I'm stuck with Richard Noggin all day. The little bastard has been curled up in the center of Cody's yellow blankets. As much I want to despise the evil bastard, I have equal amounts of respect for him. He's protecting his girl.

I sit up and head downstairs before I get lost in "what could have been" and "should be." I take a peek at the marinated steaks in the fridge then grab the ingredients for my special potato casserole. Hell, it's not special. I basically throw in everything and anything that's in arm reach. Not sure how it became coined "Cody's Famous Spuds," but I decide to make them for my girls. Yeah, that's right—my girls. I give myself that right because in my heart they are.

"Fancy" by Iggy blares throughout the house speakers as I slice and dice the potatoes and whip together all the ingredients I can scavenge out of Bertie's fridge. She has just enough milk, cheese, butter, and spices to make this masterpiece acceptable. Once I get the dish in the oven, I know it's about time to meet Cody at the bus. I go for the door, hoping like hell the bake timer works on this oven.

The fact Bertie has gifted me time alone picking up her daughter at the bus stop is pretty damn huge. It seems fast since being introduced to Cody. The thing is Bertie and I have known each other for years. We keep moving forward. It makes me incredibly happy and fearful at the same time. Once I buckle Scotty's harness—he's gone after me at least six times with his shark fangs—I get the little bastard secured and attached to the leash. I'm not sure what else a little girl needs besides her Chihuahua and new best friend picking her up at the bus stop.

"Be a good little Richard Noggin," I grumble at Scotty as I make my way to the door. "Or I'll dick punch you. Yeah, don't be going thinking you've grown on me, you little bastard."

I do my best, getting all my foul language out of my soul before leaving the house. I hear a noise the same moment I open the door, knowing I'm minutes away from scooping a brave little girl named Cody off the bus.

However, when I swing open the door with Scotty trailing at my heels, I don't meet a church-going person knocking. Hell no. I come face to face with a person I never want to see again.

"How damn ironic!" He takes a step back.

I have no words, but I'm not about to back down from this prick. "Can I help you?"

A hearty chuckle escapes him. "You can't help me, but how damn insane the same guy answering her door is about to get her ass fired."

I clear my throat and pull back the barking Scotty, who is about to rip into this dick's ankle and piss on him at the same time. I'm half tempted to let the dog have some fun. "Did you need something, Garrett?"

I swear to baby Jesus, Zeus, the Easter Bunny, and Satan that it takes all of me to keep my energy contained.

He flips his crisp collar and nods. "Bertie. I need Bertie."

Son of a bitch, I have so many comebacks, but I hear the roar of the bus and know I have more important business. This puke can flake off with the downpour of snow that hasn't stopped.

I shove past him with the dog in tow. It doesn't matter it's a damn Chihuahua and I feel like I'm trotting out my damn pit bull in a neon yellow harness I purchased off Amazon, and that I slipped on Bertie's lavender slides, knowing I was just gonna trot to the bus stop. Cody will race in with Scotty on her heels. That's how it goes, but not today.

Garrett shoves me, and I do my best catching myself on the side of the house, avoiding falling on my ass.

"Where is she?" he seethes.

"At work," I reply, caging my intense anger. I want nothing more than to tear into this prick, but I'm trying to be the bigger person here.

"God, you're a funny little prick. Wait, more like a piece of white trash." He shoves me again, and I've never felt like a bigger punk. I've never walked away from a fight. Hell, I've started them for the hell of it in the past. Christ, I'm a little puss.

She's mine, and I will fight to keep her and Cody.

It takes me a few seconds to recollect my bearings, and that's when I remember the words I told Cody. Scotty is on point, wrapping himself around a damn cement flower pot. I take it upon myself to whip and yank his leash until the metal clasps nail Garrett in the side of the head.

I swear it takes him a second or two to figure out what in the hell is going on. Fucking Scotty doesn't listen, forcing my hand to whip the leash a few more times, and for shit sakes, it nails Garrett in the face again.

"Again." Garrett stands straight, pressing his hand to the bleeding on the side of his head. "Where in the hell is Roberta?"

"If you don't know where she is, then I'm thinking it's none of your concern." Scotty lifts his leg, but I tug him back, thinking the blood streaming down the side of Garrett's face is enough.

"Well played, you low life little puke. So glad you came back into her life only to make her lose her job. I'll go find her and bring her back to me. Roberta is deemed for great things, and scum like you have no place in her life. She'll chose her job over you." He shakes his head. "I can't believe she even blinked once over you."

Ignore the douche. Ignore him. I repeat these two phrases over and over. If I told Cody she has to block out the taunts of dumbass douches, I can too.

"Cody."

I turn around at the sound of my name. The cocky bastard tucks his hand in his tailored pockets and smiles at me.

"You do know she was told by the board of the hospital if she didn't stand down in your case, she'll be fired, right?" He jerks his chin. "I'd suggest getting the hell out of her life before you ruin everything she's worked for."

I nod slowly and rub the stubble on my jawline while yanking my barking guard dog back.

"Fuck you," I grumble, not having any other words for the dickhead. I try to process his words but am unable to. It's all too fucking insane. I swear to hell if I was home in my bar, I'd be cracking open a bottle of vodka and downing the entire thing, no mixers needed.

The roar of the bus engine gains my attention, and

even though Scotty continues to bark non-stop, I go for what matters. The little blonde crazy-haired girl. The new bus driver waves at me with a tinge of apology. I'd never take out my anger on the new bus driver. It took one call to Jules to find out the legality of kicking a kid off the bus, and it seems a kindergarten squabble didn't qualify. And the crotchety old bitch that used to man the big yellow bus was canned, and Cody was once again back on the bus. I guess the old hag had two strikes and was afraid of her third.

"Who is that, Junior?" Cody hitches her thumb over her shoulder, drawing attention to the sleek, fancy car.

"No idea." I shrug, following her into the house. "Must have missed their turn."

"Wait." She freezes. "Was it Garrett?"

I don't miss the way her nose scrunches up and happy features morph into sorrow.

I nod, not being able to lie to her.

"Junior." She grabs my hand, yanking on it. I give her my full attention. "I hate, hate him. Mom says I can't use that word, but he's so mean."

"Yeah, he's a dick." I squeeze her hand. "That bad word is between us."

"He never liked me."

"His loss." I bite my bottom lip, stopping myself from calling Garrett all sorts of damn words. "He's a loser."

Dinner flies by once Bertie returns home. We all chow down on the simple cuisine I made. You'd think I was a damn world top chef as the two devour the meal. I clean up the simple mess while Bertie and

Cody escape upstairs. It takes me longer than usual rubbing out the stiffness while getting use to my new hardware. I've done a damn good job masking the pain so far.

I hang the dish towel over the faucet, eye the drying dishes, and head upstairs. I take the steps slower tonight, knowing damn well the women in my life have worn me the hell out. I stand still at the top of the stairs, hearing sweet voices sing a tender song.

"Can Junior tuck me in?"

"Honey, he's cleaning up dinner," Bertie responds. "Snuggle down under your blankets and think good thoughts."

"I'm trying, Mom, but your old boy toy, Garrett, showed up today."

Bertie's laugh echoes out into the hallway. "You've listened to Nell way too much."

"I'm serious, Mom, Garrett showeded up, and Junior ignored him. I was so proud."

Jesus, that little girl guts me around every corner. She's a tiny storm, and you never know when the skies will bust wide open.

"Did Garrett say anything to you?" Bertie asks.

"Nope. He was in his car when I hopped off the bus." There are sounds of rustling, then Cody is talking again. "My new bus driver is so, so, so nice, and Belle doesn't even look at me."

"Oh, yeah," Bertie responds, but the faraway tone of her voice lets me know she's deep in thought. I don't need to see her face to know that little fact.

"Yep, Mom, I got a real bad cramp."

Scotty takes it upon himself to bark at this moment. The little fucker doesn't stop yapping until both girls are sitting up in bed. I blink once then twice, searing a mirage before me. A sea of blonde wild curls comes into view. Scotty knocks open the door, yipping like he's hurt until he's in Cody's lap and I'm here standing in the middle of the doorway.

"Good boy." Cody pets the top of his head. Bertie continues staring at me. It's then I realize I tossed my shirt in the washer with the other t-shirts Bertie threw in.

"Junior, come tuck me in." Cody waves me in as Scotty growls at her hand.

I nod and enter the room.

Simple, innocent, peaceful eyes coax me in. She pats her tiny hand on her bed. I obey her command, perching on the side. She has me as well trained as Richard Noggin.

"Tuck me in with Mom, please, please, please?"

I relax down on the edge of the bed. Cody pats the edge of her yellow pillow. I lie back down on it and stare at the ceiling as she finishes up her jabbering.

"Junior, do you want to be thankful for anything?"

"What's that?" I roll my head, coming face to face with two beauties staring at me.

Bertie explains. "Every night we share something we are thankful for before…"

As her words trail off, Cody's fire right up. "Before we say goodnight to my daddy."

Her chubby finger points at the picture frame between us and the nightstand. I reach over, grabbing the framed photo while studying the man behind the glass. His smile is kind, similar to Cody's. She looks so much like Bertie yet so similar to her father.

"I'm thankful for…" I clear my throat, tamping

down the emotions. "I'm thankful for your daddy, Cody."

"Uh?" She perches up on my chest, staring up at me. "I don't understand."

I try again to convey what I'm feeling in this moment. "I'm thankful for this man right here." I tap the front of the photo frame. "He put you in my life, and it's been the best gift ever."

"Weird." She scrunches up her nose. "I'm thankful that we had chicken nuggets at school for lunch today."

"Chicken nuggets?" I roll over on my side, propping my head up with my hand and poking her in the ribs. "Chicken nuggets and not steak? Something is wrong with you, kid."

"Stop, Junior, stop." Cody takes a few minutes to catch her breath before rolling on her back, glancing over at her mom. "It's your turn."

Bertie screws up her lips, deep in thought. "I'm thankful for this."

"What's this?" Cody asks.

"This." She waves her arm around in the air. "Us all being here."

"Weird." Cody shakes her head and then continues to ask Scotty what he's thankful for. The damn dog on cue licks her face, causing her to giggle.

"Time for bed," Bertie announces. I pass the picture to Cody and listen as she tells her daddy good night.

The act is so honest and touching that I find my eyes stinging. I leave the room, giving the duo some time alone. I perch on the side of my bed in my dark room. It's insane how lonely it is in here, considering the two of them are just across the hall.

I hear Bertie slip from Cody's room. Her silhouette pauses right outside my door. I swear I can hear her internal thoughts. A matter of seconds pass before she turns toward her bedroom.

Garrett's words cycle over and over until there's so much raging energy built up inside of me that I can't sit still. I have to talk to her, and that's exactly what I do. *Should've tossed on a shirt* is the last thought that goes through my head as I push open the door.

"Bertie," I whisper into the room, trying not to be too loud.

I hear a grunt, and then a door in her room opens. She steps out of her en suite bedroom with her messy hair piled on top of her head. Tiny-ass shorts barely cover her, and the damn tight white tank top leaves nothing to the imagination.

"Just a sec," she slurs around the toothbrush, holding up a finger.

I don't have any willpower for shit and am about to turn and run when she appears again, drying her hands off on a pale blue towel.

"You okay?" She tilts her head. "Is something wrong?"

She's glowing beauty in this moment, lit up by the backlight of her bathroom. I'd pollute it with mention of her earlier visitor. I slowly shake my head "no" while making my way to her. With no words, I walk her backwards with my chest pressed against her sweet softness until her back meets the wall.

I force my hands to plant on the plaster of the wall so I don't ravage the hell out of her. The tension has been multiplying in leaps and bounds with each interaction, glance, and smile. I'm only a man and have run out of self-control.

I nuzzle my nose along the length of her slender neck, soaking in everything Bertie Cooper.

"Cody," she exhales, placing her hands on my back, running them up and down.

I wait for the rest of her thought, but it never comes. I bring my head down, grazing my lips over hers. They part for me, an open invitation to take what I need. It's more than a need. It's a stirring, a craving, my lifeline.

"How was work?" I press my lips to hers for our first chaste kiss before giving her a chance to answer.

"Fine." It's a one-word answer, and I need to know what she means. I may have been absent from her life for years, but I know she prides herself in her work and would shine talking about it. This solidifies all of Garrett's accusations. On one hand, it pisses me off that's she's keeping it from me. But on the other hand, I swell with pride, knowing she'd stand up to anyone to help. The intense anger at the thought of her losing her job combined with the intense attraction and adoration for this woman explodes into a beautiful mess.

"I don't want to stop," I whisper, moving my hands down her sides until they rest on the top of her hips. "I want more, Bertie. I need a longer kiss. I need it all, and if I start, I won't be able to stop."

This all comes out with the slip of a tongue, even knowing damn well the hard conversation will come afterward. I will get answers about the shit Garrett was slinging, and if she'll allow me, I'll be by her side fighting with her.

Bertie's answer is not the one I was expecting. It sure as hell is the one I was hoping for. She leans closer, darting her tongue out between her plump full lips, letting it dance along the seam of mine. She's cute and coy playing with me right now. I let her control it all. She has more to lose than me. I gave us away, and now she's offering herself up to me again and that I'll hold onto forever.

She deepens the kiss, our tongues remembering the familiar dance. It brings me back to life with a zap straight down my spine. She pushes on my chest. Following her prompt, I back up until my legs hit the side of the bed. I tumble backward, keeping her perfect body pressed to mine until we are lying on the mattress. Her body covers mine, and my hands roam every inch of her. My self-constraint tears apart in a matter of seconds. My hands sneak under her shirt. Her flesh sears my palms, and that's enough of a snap to throw me into full force.

I roll her over, stripping her clothes off until she's bare before me. I take a second to soak in her rare beauty. The Bertie I once knew is no longer there. Her body is so much more now, perfect in every way. Her creamy skin and full breasts fill my every need. I suck, lick, and roam all over her body. I get lost in her, having no idea how much time has gone by.

"More now," she pleads, her body writhing against mine.

"Not yet," I murmur against her skin.

I snake down her body, licking and sucking every inch of her skin until I'm causing her body to buck up in the air. She masks her screams as whispers while tugging on my hair. When she bursts in my mouth, her body goes lax.

"You are fucking incredible, baby." I lick back up her body until I'm kissing the hell out of her again.

She reaches down between us, causing me to hiss when she grabs me through my sweatpants.

I drop my head to her forehead, close my eyes, and say the toughest words I've ever had to speak in my life. "Baby, no. I think we tested the limits far enough tonight."

She doesn't listen, sneaking her hand down inside the waistband. Bertie was always a stubborn one when it came to something she wanted. Before I know it, my boxers are pushed down over the globes of my ass and she's lining us up.

"Bertie." I drop my elbows to frame the side of her face and press my lips to her forehead. "Slow down."

"No." She surges her hips up. "I need you, Cody. God, if I'm honest with myself, I've needed you for years. Please."

"Condom," I pant out, centimeters away from taking her.

"Pill, and I trust you."

Those last three words are my kryptonite. She trusts me. In her own right, she could have so many questions. Ask how many women there have been, but she doesn't. She's damn right to trust me. There've been other women but never unprotected. Went through a gamut of tests before my surgery and, hell, maybe she knows this little fact, but it doesn't diminish the ray of light she just gifted me.

I don't ask any more questions as our bodies blend

together. It feels like the first and last time we were ever together. All those memories come rushing back, melding together with current ones. It's blinding, gripping my heart in a tight vice, piercing me alive. When her hands grip my back, her nails sinking in, I'm brought straight back to reality. The image of what lies ahead of me is crystal clear, and I'd give up everything back home to be front and center in that picture frame.

Chapter 13

Cody

"Get your cute little butt out the door." I scoop Scotty up in my arms. "I've got this Richard Noggin."

Bertie shoots a glare my direction. "That's a silly name. Please quit calling my daughter's dog that, Junior."

I cover up my smile, knowing Bertie is on the edge of laughter herself.

"Okay, meet me at the bus again, please, please, and bring Scotty." Cody claps her hands in front of her, jumping up and down, with her canary yellow Doc Marten boots the brightest part of her outfit. "I've been so good I get to ride all week."

"It's a date, Missy." I ruffle the top of her wild curls. She doesn't bat me away or worry if I messed up her hair. It's what I love most about this little ray of light. She loves life and that alone.

"Yes!" She fists pumps the air. "Mom, let's go.

We can't be late. I have Smarty breakfast this morning."

Bertie smiles brightly down at her daughter. I learned the other day that Smarty breakfast is a super, super cool club where a teacher eats with you. Bertie later explained it's a small learning group where the students feel special. It seems to be doing the trick.

I laid next to Bertie last night until she fell asleep. Snuck out of her room like I was in damn high school. I didn't get a wink of sleep. Remained wide awake all night, not wanting to lose a second of the memories we'd just made. I must have dozed off around six in the morning because Bertie woke me up with sweet minty kisses peppered on my scruff. She has blocked me from shaving for days now.

"I have to go into work for a few, then I'll be home." Bertie brushes a light kiss against my cheek, not hiding a thing from her daughter. Cody is smart enough to know her mother wouldn't bring a complete stranger into her house and let him live here. Or that's what I tell myself.

"Get your cute butts in gear." I reach down, groping her ass as she races out of the house.

I don't get to relish the touch and enjoy the sensation stirring in my sweats thanks to the dog sent straight from hell. Scotty takes it upon himself to nip at my fingers, getting me away from his girls. And I guarantee that's exactly what he intended to do.

I watch as my two golden hair beauties disappear into the white wintery scene then into their car. I remain in place until their tail lights disappear. I go through my PT routine, working myself as hard as I can. I don't stop until I'm exhausted but know better than to push too far beyond that point of pain. I did that a few times in the hospital, trying my damnedest to get the point across that I was fine to the physical therapist and to Bertie. It was one of the dumbest decisions I ever made.

I never knew "cheeking" a pill was a term, but I do know. Nurse Ratchet made sure to explain that term to me while in the hospital. Little did she know I was cheeking the hell out of the pills and she had no idea what was going on. Bertie never thought about asking. I'd feel low if the pills were fighting some infection-type shit, but they were mere painkillers and I didn't need them. I haven't spent much time dwelling on the fact that my heart stopped beating and I was brought back to life. Instead of doing that, I've lived each freaking second as my last.

Cliché as hell, but in my story it's reality.

Today there's no knock on the door as I finish marinating some chicken. Nope, that thing blows right open with a little hurricane also known as Nell whipping in. I glance over my shoulder, sealing up the bag with the marinade and chicken breast. I don't have a chance to speak before she's ripping my ass. A huge smile engulfs my face as I remember the same damn spitfire from college. She hasn't changed a bit.

"Playing house." She cocks a hip on the island, glaring me down. "Seems mighty fine to be strolling back in here, picking up after the messy years of Bertie's life."

I don't respond, knowing damn well she doesn't want a response and isn't anywhere near done with her rant. I let her go on because I just know she's about to spill all the beans. Hell, it's what she's known for. We used to call her the Bean Spiller for a darn good reason. She could never keep a secret, and I'm talking from presents to simple surprise visits.

"I'm the one who held her for months. Damn near a year after your dumbass excuse and Bethany's explanation. It was me." She pounds her chest. "Then it was me who held little Cody while she grieved the death of her father. And just so you know, I was totally against that dumb name. Nearly ruined our friendship over that argument."

By this point, I drop the bag of marinating lemon basil chicken breast on the counter and face her, crossing my arms over my chest. I know I am going to get all the information, and the war is just beginning.

"And it was me who held her and ate tacos with her when you tried to go dying like some fucking hero. Yeah, it was me. Then she told me you were moving in and I bit my damn tongue, but no, it's gone too far. Way too far. The hospital has a case against her. She's a few days away from being fired. And you, Romeo," she steps up to me, jabbing my chest with her pointer finger, "are about to get her ass fired. You just had to go and open the door, giving Garrett his final pieces of ammunition."

She thumps out each word with a jab to my chest. I follow each of her words, but it takes me seconds to process them. Nell doesn't pick up on this cue and of course carries on.

"She visited you every single day in the ICU. Sang you songs from that dumb playlist. Checked and rechecked your charts, never giving up. The day you woke up, she was there. You wouldn't respond to anything but her voice and touch. She wouldn't let go. You were the only thing that mattered. Even when she was told to stand down, she refused. Flung that gaudy ring in Garrett's face several days earlier. He told her she'd regret it. And when she wouldn't leave your side, his promise was cemented."

Nell finally takes a breath then plucks a carrot from the veggie tray I cut up and swipes the bright orange vegetable through the creamy homemade ranch. I take advantage of her hollow stomach and begin asking my own questions.

"He threatened her? She's losing her job? What in the hell?" It's all a tornado of questions as I put Nell's words into a string of coherent thought.

"She didn't tell you, did she?" Nell drops her gaze.

"For all that is holy, can we quit saying that? There's no more 'he didn't tell you' or 'she didn't tell you' in this story. I need to know what in the hell is going on before it's too late. I made one huge dumbass catastrophic mistake, and I'm not about to make another."

"She'll let you," she responds.

"She'll let me what?" I pound my fist into the top of the counter.

"She'll let you make that mistake because Bertie always saves herself."

I wring out the pain throbbing in my knuckles. "Bullshit. She doesn't need to save herself. I'll testify to anything she needs me to. I damn well know and so does everyone else at that hospital that she did not want to operate on me. She practically sang it to my entire floor."

"You don't get it." Nell shakes her head. "Bertie has made it this far and doesn't need you to save her. She's made her choices, and now she will be the one to defend them. Do you really think the true Roberta Cooper would've stood by your side when she knew her job was on the line just for old time sakes? Think about it. She did it because of her love for you, and I, for one, will never understand it."

I remain silent, growing more pissed off with each second ticking by.

"She's conquered mountains, and this, my friend, is a simple mole hole. So you can stay here and push to be by her side, which in essence makes you a Garrett in my book, or you can let her fight like the woman she is and see where the pieces land."

I ease my weight onto my other leg. "So let me get this straight. You are telling me to walk away from her?"

"Like I said, put the pieces together, Cody."

"Walk away is what you're saying?" I press once again. I know damn well what she's laying down, and honestly, I get it. It's my Bertie. The person she is. As hard as it is to swallow, I understand it.

"Figure it out, Einstein." She shakes her head. "Hell, that's too big of a compliment for you. I meant duck nugget. Yeah." She stands more confident. "Figure it the hell out, duck nugget."

"Do you mean dick nugget?" I shake my head. "I'm not really sure where you're going with this."

Nell steps over to the marinating chicken and points. "Toss a few of those in a bag for me to take home. I've got a hell of a lot of work to pound out tonight and love me some chicken."

I can't keep up with this chick. She hates me. Sort of kind of appraises me in one sentence and tells me to walk away. I have nothing left to do but bag up the freaking chicken and send her on her merry way home.

"Here." I slap the bag in her direction. Nell grabs it without blinking. There go the leftovers for my lunch tomorrow. It's worth the sacrifice to get her the hell out of here.

"Thanks, old pal." She pats my chest and whirls on her heels for the front door, but before she leaves, of course she has to have the last word.

"Since I don't have time to draw out a picture for you, think about it this way, buddy. You walked into her life at one point and changed everything then walked out, giving her no choice on the matter. And now you've waltzed right back in yet again, giving her no choice. And by all rights, the way things are going, you can stay and save the day, taking everything right back away from Bertie, or you can leave and put the ball in her court."

And with that, the front door slams shut. I let her words sink in deep in my gut like a boat anchor. As much as I'd like to admit that Nell is just a hater, I can't. She's right. Nell hit the nail on the head. No matter how much chemistry Bertie and I have and the amount of love we've untangled and woven from the years we were separated, she's still right. It's time for Bertie to make the decision, not me. I don't get to engage in her fight. It's up to her, and I'll give her that.

I slump in the dining room chair, letting everything settle in. It stings and hurts like a dirty bitch, and I'm thankful I have a bottle of pain pills up in my room. There will be no cheeking any of them in my near future. I'll need all the courage I can get.

A muted sound sings out through Bertie's home. I follow the sound until I discover the culprit. Bertie's cellphone. The number isn't saved as a contact. It's just a scrambled-up mix of numbers. I stand and stare at it. Just when the light begins to dim and the ringing has ceased, it lights up again with a text. I squint, reading the words I can make out on the preview screen.

Unknown: Bertie, it's Martin McDouglas. Nice meeting you today. Your case is strong. Keep doing what you're doing and I'll be in contact soon.

It doesn't take a rocket scientist to know that Martin McDouglas is a lawyer and that's where Bertie spent her day. Nell's words weigh on me the rest of the afternoon. I'm not too proud to say I found what I can assume is Nell's and Bertie's stash of wine and vodka. I'm not that big of an idiot to take wine from women, so I pound a few gulps of vodka, just enough to give me that slight buzz that makes my head swim. The liquid does its magic, numbing all of me until I fall onto the couch and into a peaceful slumber with Scotty curled at my side as I pet the little devil who became a caring, kind dog in my eyes. The few shallow swallows of vodka put me right off into a nap, which is way better than sitting here worrying the rest of the day away.

Chapter 14

Bertie

The meeting with the lawyer was exhausting, the kind of tired you can feel in your bones. It drained me physically and mentally, even though everything sounded very positive. Mr. McDouglas encouraged me we had a robust case if the witness list I provided was strong enough. His track record helps reassure me as well. My bank account, on the other hand, wasn't so impressed. However, if everything turns out the way I want, that money will be right back in my account.

This situation didn't have the time to hire the doctor's association I'm in. Nope, no way in hell will I or would I ever let my hard work, determination, sweat, pride, and tears be erased by an egomaniac. My parents taught me better, and they'd be damn proud. They're enjoying their retirement over in Ireland, and I'd never ruin it with this mess I got caught up in. Not a chance. Some may call me bullheaded, but I like to think I'm a strong-willed, determined woman, and that's exactly what I want my sweet, little Cody to grow up to be, no matter what she chooses to pursue.

Pulling into my garage, I feel myself being re-energized with the thought of what's waiting for me on the other side. No matter how bad life can be, the world has brought my greatest love back into my life, and that's enough to make me smile again. I swear every part of my body and soul has blossomed back to life. He's everything, and I have no idea what the future holds.

My phone dings as I enter the kitchen. I left the damn thing lying on the counter. On autopilot, I pick it up and swipe it to life. Big, big mistake.

Garrett: Stubborn damn woman. I knew there was something about you that I couldn't resist and I guess that was breaking you down. No lawyer will help you in this case. You have two options. Get fired and go before the board hoping like hell your license isn't stripped away or put that ring back on your finger.

What the hell? I knew Garrett carried an air of arrogance, but this is so off the mark I can't even begin to understand it. He was always kind and gentle with me, yeah, a bit overbearing when it came to showing me off, but this isn't the man I thought I knew. A new message appears.

Garrett: And really, moving the man into your house? I can't even begin to comprehend your stupidity, Roberta.

I react on instinct, racing back out to my car. Call me crazy, but I don't want his venom in my house in any shape or form. What's happening under my roof is beautiful magic, and I want to keep that bottled up as long as I can. I settle in my car, rereading the texts. My head bounces on the headrest. I repeat the action over and over. This man is bound and determined to take me down if I don't bend to his will. Why in the ever-loving hell would he want to be with a woman who he has grown to despise in such a short time?

My phone vibrates in my hand as the ringtone goes off. I don't have to look at it to know who is calling. Avoiding him hasn't worked in my favor so far.

"Hello." My voice shakes, only making me more pissed off at the situation.

"Roberta." His deep, seductive voice comes through the other line. "Didn't think you'd answer."

"Well, I did." I run my hands through my hair. "What's your game? What in the hell is this all about?"

"I've been pretty damn clear, Roberta. I want you as my wife."

"What in the hell, Garrett?" I pound the steering wheel, avoiding the horn. "We dated for a few months, you popped the question catching me off guard, you can't stand my daughter, so what in the hell gives?"

"You. That's what gives. I need to get married. You're perfect for me. Your story will win so many hearts, and then having me as your husband will be the cherry on the top."

"Are you sick, Garrett? None of this makes sense."

"I have to get married, and like you said, I wasted months on you, Roberta. You lose your license or marry me."

"Fuck off." The two words rolling off my tongue free and exhilarate me. "Garrett, you don't win here, and you may think you're smart and have everything tidied up in the palms of your hands. You are wrong. Money, Mommy, and Daddy won't save you this time. I suggest you stop before this gets really messy."

His only reply is a deep hearty chuckle from the other end.

"Laugh now, Garrett, but I've been keeping track of all the harassment from you, and I'm not the only one with a list."

I don't wait for his reply, ending the call and promptly blocking his number. I don't stop there, powering down my phone. I'm home and the only two people who truly matter are waiting inside for me.

The house is silent when I enter, like it was before. I let out a long exhale, thankful no one heard me. I ignore it, placing the milk in the fridge and bread in the pantry, then make my way upstairs. It's a routine even though there's no need to shower or take five minutes of alone time. I do it anyway, avoiding the shower but jumping into yoga pants and a comfy tee. I'm at the point to taking off my bra with Cody around. I mean, hell, the man licked every square inch of my body and brought me to life like I've never experienced before, but I decide to keep it on. Might be the last piece of armor I need when it comes to him. Like I ever had a chance. I'm the only joker in that scene.

"Cody." I trot back down the stairs, having no idea where he is.

"In here," his voice responds.

I startle, jumping back when Cody's profile appears in the kitchen. The same room I just walked through.

"You scared the shit out of me." I keep my hand over my chest. "It's like you disappeared into the shadows and reappeared. I didn't see you when I came in."

He shrugs. "I was napping on the couch."

"Well, hell, you're like a superhero, being all stealthy and shit." I walk toward him. "How was your day? Did you take your meds? And do your stretches?"

I shake my head slightly, knocking away the damn doctor mode, but I can't help myself. It's embedded in my DNA.

"Yes, yes, and yes. I've checked all the above boxes," he mutters, taking a bag of marinated chicken from the fridge.

"Are you okay, Cody?" I stutter in my step, getting closer to him yet knowing something is off.

He turns to stare at me. There's silence slicing between us. I'm not sure what to make of it, but I'm not about to turn away. There's an eerie brilliance of evil brewing levels below us, but it always has. We both know it—two kids from the wrong sides of the track. Bertie's parents worked their damn ass off to

137

get her into the college of her dreams. Her tattered jeans and worn Chucks were glaringly obvious to anyone studying the social classes of our hometown. Two kids from the wrong sides of the classroom yet we always magnetized to one another. There was no exception once we entered the same plane.

"I'm fine." He steps toward me. "Tough day on me doing everything to recover."

I'm not an idiot. I know there's so much more behind his words. I don't have the courage to ask about it, falling back on my training as a doctor.

"Are you feeling okay?" I step closer, as if we are calling each other out in a high-stakes poker game. "How was your temperature? Did it spike? You know that's not a good sign."

"Oh yeah." He smirks, closing the distance between us with his large palm tugging my hip towards him. "It spiked."

"Yeah?" I trail a finger down his jawline.

"It did." He pulls me closer. "It's weird. It happened the moment you walked into your own kitchen. Something really strange happened, Doc."

I throw my head back and laugh hard until my stomach hurts. "You're so cheesy, and like I've said a thousand times, some things never change."

"The greatest singer once said," he pauses and smirks, "just shut up and kiss me, or as others like to say, a long story straight."

And that's when it happens—all the wrongs in the world are righted as Cody's full sexy lips cover mine. We move in unison with all the worries in the world erasing at once. Hands roam and clothes shed. Cody admires my body just as he did last night and the first time we were together and the same way he made love to me the night before he walked out of my life.

The passion and angst simmering deep down in my core out-powers my previous thoughts. Cody wipes away every single thought and worry with each move of his body against mine. It's magic, the purest sense of voodoo, so intense I'm hypnotized sucking in and memorizing each move. I'm so entranced in him that I don't blink when he winces in pain. I'm too entranced in us to listen to my doctor brain. He's giving me all of him, and I'm soaking all of it in. What we are doing is so much more than science. It's more than life. It's everything.

***

We remain breathless on the floor of the entryway hall as the timer on my phone and his go off at the same time.

"The bus," he whispers against my temple.

"The bus." I clench his back.

As much as it pains me, I pry myself from Cody's body. It isn't easy as we are tangled as if you don't know where one begins and the other one ends. It's a struggle in itself to gather all of our clothes.

"Hey, Cody." I tug my tee over my head, swiping my hair out in a fan before glancing over at him. "Thank you."

He stills, processing those two words more than he needs to. I watch as his thick throat gulps down. The awkward tension is back. I know beyond the black and white print in any textbook or medical file that he's keeping something back. The pain is written on his features, and I want nothing more than to wipe it away.

"For what?" Two simple words.

"For being you," I respond.

He chucks up his jeans, fastening them, then has me in his arms again, our foreheads pressed against each other as he stares me down.

"Letting me back in and sharing everything with me you've worked so damn hard to gain." He tilts his head, kissing my temple. "That's something I'll never take for granted. I'm always here for you, Bertie."

Before I have the chance to ask what in the hell is going on my phone alarm begins serenading us again. It's a beacon that tears the two of us apart. Cody grabs my hand and opens the door, leading me out to grab my girl from the bus. We don't exchange another word until the big yellow bus pulls up in front of my house.

"She's amazing, Bertie." Cody squeezes my hand, not making eye contact. "She's perfect, and don't let anyone else tell you any different."

It's acceptance and goodbye all wrapped in one. After the day I've had, I can't comprehend a damn thing. My little princess doesn't acknowledge me as she bounds off the bus and darts towards us. It's not me she goes to. With her arms wide open and a huge smile plastered on her cherubic face, she heads straight for Cody aka Junior.

"Junior, I called a kid 'pecker' in class today. The teacher didn't hear, and I guess this kid's dad calls the dog pecker all the times and then kicks at it." She smooshes Cody's face with her tiny palms. "After lastest recess, he told me he thought I was going to kick hard at him. I was just so, so mad I remembered one of your words, but now we are good friends, and I didn't even kick him. I ignored him."

Cody doesn't have to fake or mask his smile as he beams wide at her. I'm not sure how her dad would've reacted, but I do know he'd want a man like Cody in her life embracing and loving the hell out of her, even if it wasn't conventional.

"Well, good one, squirt, but let's not use that word again." He shrugs, keeping my hand in his and turning to the house. "Let's shelve that word, but damn—darn good use of it."

I get caught up on the fact Cody corrects himself every chance he gets. He has never put on a fake persona. Nope, he's been himself, teaching my daughter all kinds of naughty words and yet at the same teaching her appropriate ones.

Junior and Cody ditch me the second we enter the house. The two of them don't let the feet of snow stop them from grilling the chicken outside on the barbecue. I watch from the inside, feeling like a figurine trapped in a snow globe. It's hell, and I don't care for the feeling. I sense Cody pulling further and further away from me. It frightens and liberates me at the same time, and there's no way I can explain it.

My little girl jabbers away while jotting down in a notebook with her neon pineapple marker. The scene I'm observing is an eager waitress taking orders. Cody is the chef and customer at the same time.

"I'll take a C," he replies to something she told him.

I near the French glass doors to overhear their conversation.

"The large size or small order?" she asks, tapping the end of the marker to her chin.

"Large size of course."

"Junior." Cody giggles wildly. "You always order the large ones. I need to learn my small size letters."

"Large size." He flips the chicken on the grill then goes to her.

They continue the letter game as if they've done it their whole lives. The innocent and loving child has no idea Cody keeps flinging safe letters her way. It doesn't matter as her smile shines to life with each of his praises. She even shakes her head as he holds his hand over hers as he shows the correct way to write a letter. They continue this over and over until the chicken is cooked.

I tried my best to whip up a salad and warm some rolls all the while watching their shared interactions. Cody doesn't get frustrated at his student's backwards letters. He simply holds his large hand over hers, helping her form them correctly. Hot, searing tears form, and I do my best to fight them back. Blink by blink and slice by slice of juicy red tomatoes, I bat them away.

I've never been stuck in such a hard spot. The saying between a rock and a hard place has nothing on the predicament I've found myself in. Cody has a life five hours away, and mine is here. It's not as simple as walking away. Blood, sweat, and tears have gone into everything I've built up. I've scratched and clawed my way this far; I'm not about to go begging for help. Yeah, it's plain stupidity, but

I can't ignore it.

"Mom." Cody tugs on my t-shirt. "Why are your eyes watering?"

"Onions, silly." I wipe underneath my eyes, not even realizing those tears finally won out and spilled over.

"Um." She taps her chin and rolls her eyes. "You are chopping a tomato."

I open my mouth, but there's nothing to say. She's caught me, and one thing I've never done is lie to my girl. But there's no way I can begin to explain to her what is causing the tears.

"Must be one of those onion-possessed tomatoes." Cody scoops her up in his arms, hoisting her over his shoulder in a fireman pose.

"Junior, you're lying," she manages to get out through giggles.

"Nope, it's a real thing. They are super rare." His voice fades as he rounds the corner. "The chances of slicing into one are about one in a trillion."

She laughs louder, and I relax back on the counter. Just like our love—it's a one in a trillion chance of ever finding it again. That's something I can't let go off. It doesn't matter our lives are in different spots. I'll battle my way through to make it happen.

"Mom." Minutes later, Cody comes racing into the room. "We are making slime after dinner."

When I turn around, eyes free of tears, Cody is hefting in the largest container of Elmer's Glue I've ever seen. Junior packs in another box of shit. I have no idea what's going on.

"I'm going to practice my letters in the slime." She plops the jug on the table. "It's going to be so, so fun."

She scrambles up onto a dining room chair.

"Dinner first, missy." Junior ruffles her hair. "And that means trying everything we cooked."

She turns up her nose but finally surrenders, agreeing. To say dinner was awkward would be an understatement. Cody didn't pick up on it, rambling non-stop from topics ranging from letters to how snow melts. The only sound that comes from the adults are a few grunts and clanking of forks.

"Let's clean up the dishes, so we can get busy on the slime." Junior stands up once he's polished off all the chicken left on our plates. "Your mom can take a shower then join us."

"Yes, yes, yes." Cody bounds from her chair, actually taking her plate to the sink.

It's a rare occurrence. Actually, it's a first. I've always been so exhausted once I was able to cook a full meal and not some nuke-and-cook meal that I've never made her take her plate to the sink. The dirty dishes were always an afterthought. They'd get cleaned up one way or another.

I grab my plate and salad bowl along with the dressings. Once I place everything where each item belongs, large hands grab my hips, inching their way around to my front. It's a hot whisper on my neck that fully gains my attention.

"Go shower." Full, sexy lips trail their way up the length of my neck. "And meet us back down here."

I can't help but melt back into Cody. I let him catch me whole, relishing in his touch and presence. I'm safe and home with him here.

"Okay," I manage to stutter out.

Cody doesn't stop his sinful assault with his hands sneaking up the front of my t-shirt, grazing the underside swell of my breasts. It's the most delicious appetizer that doesn't nearly satisfy my hunger.

"Junior, I'm all ready," comes a sweet voice.

"Baby." Cody's baritone, gruff voice echoes in my ear. "Please, please tell me if you need anything."

I nod and take a long and painful gulp, relaxing my head on his shoulder. "Okay."

I stutter out each sound, feeling Cody's body go stiff behind me, ruining our sweet moment. Before I know it, our moment shatters, blowing away.

Cody has to have the last word, as he always does. "I mean it, Bertie. I'd do anything."

And he's gone and at the sink cleaning up the mess from dinner. It's a sight. I don't have it in me to process all of it. I head up to my room, indulging in that hot shower. I don't rush or race, knowing my little Cody is in safe hands. Thoughts, ideas, plans roll over on an endless loop in my mind. It's too much, and I give into the searing hot water pelting down on me. The same happens as I dry off and dress in comfortable clothes, worn, soft material that hugs my skin. I force myself to turn off my brain driving all the thinking and decide to live in the moment.

It's her sweet giggle that powers my steps down the stairs. It's her questions and Cody guiding her through the process. When I enter the kitchen, she's sitting on his lap as he reads the step by step directions. Her face is pressed against the screen with Cody moving his head around hers to continue reading. I lean on the door jamb, soaking in the moment. In the short time he's been around, my girl has fallen in love with the same man who owns my heart. She fell hard, just like her mom.

The confusion threatens to set in again. I don't let it, forcing myself to join the fun activity. I've tried damn hard to do fun things like this with Cody over the years. Unfortunately, they've been far and few between. That's where Nell stepped up, taking charge for me. Nell is just another reason why this is my home.

"Mom." Cody grabs my hand, distracting me from my vortex of self-punishment. "We are just about to get started."

She points at each ingredient, explaining the process the best she can. I continue to nervously nibble on my bottom lip, still caught up a bit in my own head.

"We're ready, Junior." Cody claps her hand.

I look up the same moment to see Cody dip his fingers in a bowl of water and flick them in my direction, the drops making contact with my face. All I can do is let my jaw hang wide open.

"Junior." Cody gasps, covering her mouth in shock.

He does it again before I react. The second round brings a smile to my face.

"Looked like you could lighten up." He shrugs, getting me for a third time.

"Stop." I laugh, wiping the droplets of water from my face.

"Are you with us now?" He shoots up an eyebrow with his smile on full display.

I nod, and the slime scene ensues. Then I spot the contact lens solution on the table and point at it. "Did you just…"

"No, babe, it's a bowl of water in case we need to wash our hands."

I nod. Then the duo snaps into action, pouring the glue into a large tub. Junior measures the baking soda, pouring it into the tub.

"Okay, mix it up." He nods to Cody. She hikes up the sleeves of her shirt and digs in.

Next in is glitter then finally the contact lens solution. Slime forms, accompanied with a high-pitch squeal from Cody. I get up from the table, pouring myself a large glass of wine. Lord knows I've deserved it today.

I rest back in the dining room chair, pulling my legs into a crisscross position until I'm comfortable. Garrett's threats dull with each sip of wine and bouts of laughter from the two in front of me.

"You okay?" Cody's sexy-as-sin lips press to my forehead. He snags my wine glass, taking a healthy sip. I don't even try to ridicule him about mixing alcohol and meds.

"Don't worry." His whisper tickles the shell of my ear. "I haven't been taking any pain meds the past few days."

I turn my face up to him. Our lips graze each other. "What? Why?"

"I don't need them." He winks, stealing a quick kiss. "I had one hell of a surgeon and feel damn good."

"Junior, look!"

And just like that, our moment is shattered and completed all at the same time.

Chapter 15

Cody

Tonight was perfect. Just a simple glimpse of what we could have. I vow to remain patient, not forcing the issue, and it's taking every strand of self-control I possess. The roads have been drivable even though it was one hell of a snow storm and snowflakes keep flurrying down every night, but I've held Jessie off. He knows what is going on but has never questioned me, allowing me to live in the moment.

"Junior."

I glance down at Cody curled up to my side as I relax back on her headboard. "Yeah, kiddo?"

"Can you read it again?" her sleepy voice asks.

"Yeah, but you need to let your mom tuck you in."

Their bedtime ritual is something that, no matter how damn selfish I want to be, I will ever interrupt or take over.

"Hand me Daddy." She perches up on her elbows,

digging hard into my ribs. I wince and hand her the picture.

I let her talk to her dad, thanking the man in the photograph for everything he's given me. Cody might not be mine or will be in my life forever, but these few weeks I've spent with her are something that can never be replaced or bought with money.

"Okay, here." She hands me the photo. "Can you read *The Story of Ferdinand* again? I really love him."

"Yeah, sweetie." I open the book to the first page again.

This was my favorite book growing up, too. My parents didn't read it to me. My nanny did. But I related to him and vowed never to give up. I have no doubt that similar thoughts race through Cody's head.

Bertie peeks her head in the door. I nod to her and pat the other side of me. She curls up behind me, reaching her hand out to grab her daughter's across my stomach. The two beauties snuggle in as I begin reading the book. I'm not too far in when light snores fill the air.

"She's out," Bertie whispers.

I peer down at the sweet girl who has her cheek pressed into my chest. "That she is."

I manage to wiggle my way out from between the two of them, the hardest thing I've had to do. Damn sure didn't want to leave their warmth. I'd sleep in that same spot for the rest of my days and be damn eternally happy.

I force myself to pad out of the room and go for a hot shower, turning the handle straight to hot. I relish in the feeling of the piercing sensation on my skin, knowing the call I need to make. It will be the hardest thing I've ever had to do. But Nell is right. This is Bertie's life, and it's time she chooses what she wants. I walked out last time, forcing her and our hands—not this time.

After drying off, the house is silent. There's a dull glow coming from Bertie's room. I know if I go to her, all my self-determination will erupt in my face. I can't go to her. With that pinch of reality, I fall back on the bed. My stirring desire for the woman who owns me comes to life in my boxers. I ignore it. Nothing will do unless it's her.

When I'm about to doze off, a rustling catches my attention. I roll over to face the door. Just a slice of light from the moon shining through the blinds gifts me the vision of Bertie raising her shirt over her head. I don't say a thing and do my best not to move. This is her power play, and I'll let her have it.

The bed dips, then her warm flesh presses against mine. One arm rests on my side while the other hand palms my cheek. No words are exchanged as we lie there in silence staring at one another. I'm shocked how the lack of words are more intoxicating than any shot of whiskey. I don't move, only letting her touch me, and I won't be the first to say a word.

It seems Bertie isn't going to be, either. She rolls her naked body on top of mine, pressing my back into the bed, dropping her forehead to my chest. Wet, tender lips kiss up and down my chest, her nails dragging along my sides. I give her my body, letting her take it all. It's hers, after all.

I don't move, getting lost in her touch, scent, and

sensation. It's everything. I never want it to end.

"Cody," she moves her lips in a whisper against mine, "I need you."

"I'm yours. Take me." I finally move, brushing her long locks from her shoulder and cupping her cheek.

And she takes it all, driving each movement. My boxers are tugged down until they fall on the floor. Bertie settles above me, her nails digging into my chest as she takes every part of me. My hands remain on her hips, digging into her flesh. I bite down on my bottom lip, the piercing pain holding my release at bay. I'm able to concentrate on the beauty riding me until she breaks to pieces, gripping me as her anchor. It's then I allow myself to lose myself in her.

She collapses on my body, not moving to get off me. My large hand moves her hair to the side, then I roam my palm up and down her perfect, creamy skin until her breathing begins to even out. Her voice startles me when I thought she was about to give in to slumber.

"I love you, Cody. I always have. You brought me to life, and it seems you still have that power. I so, so, love you with everything I have."

I lean up, placing a kiss to her forehead. "I love you, too, Bertie. I always have since the day you entered that classroom and will never stop."

With that, she's out, relaxed on top of me. I tug the blankets up, covering the tops of her shoulders and relishing in her warmth. Then I reach over and grab my cellphone, punching out the hardest words I've ever had to send.

Me: Jessie, whenever you and Max are ready.

My phone screen lights up, alerting me to a text. Thank shit, I put it on silent. I've found out Cody is a light sleeper on some nights and then passes out like a drunk on others. There's no rhyme or reason as to when she decides she can't sleep in the middle of the night. So, to play it safe, I've kept my phone on silent during the night.

Jessie: Right on, man. We'll be up there on Thursday around 4 PM.

That's two days away—too much time for me to remain firm in my decision. I know I can't wait that long.

Me: How about tomorrow?

Jessie: Someone eager to get home?

Me: Nah, just need to get back to work is all.

Jessie: Yeah, I'll make it work.

Me: See you then, dickhead. Thanks.

The bubbles at the bottom of the screen let me know he's typing back a response. It doesn't stop me from placing it face down on the nightstand.

"Ball's in your court, baby. I hope I'm enough that you choose me," I whisper into the top of her head. "Because God knows I'll cherish you the rest of my life, whether it be here or back near Boone where I live now. All that matters is that you and that precious little girl are in my life."

My eyes grow heavy with no need for whiskey or any other substance. The woman in my arms is all I need. Will ever need. But did I just lay down my own death sentence?

***

Bertie

"Play it again," Cody's sweet, giggly voice echoes across the room.

I feel around the bed, coming up with the conclusion that I'm here all by myself.

"Dude, you've listened to that song twenty times now."

"I love Brantley Gilbert."

"You've heard one song."

"Play it."

"Fine," comes a grumble.

"Are you sure you have to go home?" my daughter asks. I can imagine the two of them, picture the two of them with coloring books propped between them, yellow markers spread out everywhere accompanied with bedhead.

"Yeah, squirt. It's time."

"But you promise to visit me three times a month and do that FaceTime thing?"

"I thought it was two times a month?"

"You said three. I double swear pinky promise. I don't lie."

153

Cody's rumble of laughter fills the air. "Okay, three visits a month plus FaceTime calls."

"Look, I remember how to do them." There's a slight pause. "Why did someone send you this picture?"

Cody's gruff cough then the sound of scrambling gains my full attention. I tip-toe to peer in the room just in time to see Cody get his phone back and my girl staring at him with questions in her eyes.

"Uh…my friend Brady sent it to me." That's all he has to offer.

"He's very bad. That's really bad, Junior."

"Yes, it is. I'm going to kick his… Nevermind, he needs to learn some things."

Cody plucks the phone from his hand. "So, it's this button then this one."

"Yeah." He nods.

"Let's go wake up Mom, to make sure she has your number." She hops from the bed. "It's about school time anyway." My little girl waves me off.

I take several big steps back, brushing my hair back as if I was about to come out of my room to wake her up.

"Oh good, Mom." She races up to me. "Cody has to go home today, but we are still gonna be bestest friends."

She proceeds to tell me everything I already overhead. I scoop up my girl and hug the hell out of her while wanting to cry into her soft golden hair. I don't remain strong in my own fight. Cody rounds the corner, and the moment we make eye contact, he doesn't have to tell me he's leaving. I can read it in his sorrowful expression and in the grief dancing in his eyes. We are only half a chapter from our ending.

It's a trial getting Cody dressed and on the bus. She remained glued to her hero's side, continuing to ask him over and over if their promise was still good. I know she has no idea what is about to happen. There's no way she could possibly sink it all in at her age. Hell, I can't even digest all of it.

Little Cody and Scotty play on the floor while I fill up my traveling coffee mug for the road. Typically, I'm scavenging for hot coffee, and most of the time it's cold and tastes like shit at the hospital. I've grown used to having a hot pot ready for me courtesy of him. Jesus, every thought and everything I do involves him. Always has.

"Going into work today?" Cody leans back on the counter, crossing his arms over his chest, laying down a clear-cut boundary.

The lie slices my mouth wide open. "Yeah, just for a few hours."

I don't know how to put my thumb on it, but I can tell he knows I'm full of shit. I have another meeting with my lawyer and hoping like hell a few nurses show up as well. I had no idea how dark Garrett was until yesterday when a few came forward, not to mention his texts and call.

"Bertie." His features relax. "Do you need anything from me?"

It's not the first time he's asked this in a roundabout way, and it's not lost upon me he's prying for more or at the least a morsel of information.

"I don't know." I shake my head, staring down at my shoes. I hear his large feet making their way in my direction and still don't have the courage to glance up. I'm a coward. It's so ironic. I spent years hating him for being the same thing and yet here I stand.

"Bertie." He cups my jaw, urging me to look up at him. His other hand tangles in my hair, tilting my head. "Talk to me."

"I'm lost," I whisper.

"Let me help you." He drops his forehead to mine. "Please."

"I can't."

I feel his body holding me tense, then he snarls at me. "Why?"

"Because," I let out a huff of frustration, "I don't know what in the hell I'm doing."

"Let me help you. I'm yours and you are mine." He presses his lips to mine not kissing me, but kissing me all at the same time. "I'm here, and it doesn't matter if it's here, there, or anywhere."

We both erupt in laughter at the same time. He shakes his head.

"Damn, I sound like Dr. Seuss these days."

"That you do." This time I press my lips to his, stealing a kiss I need to power me on. Cody Sterling may not know nor have the patience for it, but one way or the other, I'll make my way back to him.

"Mom, we need to go!" A sweet voice interrupts our moment, followed by devil dog's yipping, screeching barks.

"Just a second," I holler over my shoulder then look right in Cody's eyes. "I've felt love like this one other time, and it's for my girl out there. Please trust me."

He nods, swallowing down a retort. I know it's taking every ounce of self-control he possesses not to give me what's on his mind. I never thought coming full circle would be so damn brutal.

"I will. Trust me."

I seal one final kiss to his lips, knowing he'll be long gone by the time I make it back home. The day ahead of me is daunting and may just be my undoing.

He tugs me closer, tucking my head into his chest and squeezing me with all he has. I melt into him as if he is warmth and I'm freezing.

"Don't let me go, Bertie." He kisses the top of my head. "I'm going to walk away because that's what I should do."

"This isn't goodbye," I murmur into his chest, inhaling his scent. It's one I could smell the rest of my days.

"Mom! I have to get there for my breakfast learning!"

My daughter's demand pulls me away. I feel each step with a threatening bone deep tug, as if I'm trudging through sludge that brings me down with each stride. I continue forward, leaning on my daughter's energy and zest for life. I'm doing this to teach her what strong women are made of. The love of my life is right here willing to give me the world again, yet another man is threatening to take away everything I've fought so hard for. I have to stand up and fight the good fight, then go to the man my heart has always belonged to.

"Mom, the light is green!" Cody squeals in the backseat in her booster seat. "Pedal to the medal, woman!"

I grin, loving hearing a part of Cody in her. The grin that graces my face even wears me out. I swear it's been the stress of the last few months that have been catching up to me. There's no time for the weary in the heat of the battle. Garrett will go down.

Chapter 16

Cody

"I get you." I ruff up the top of Scotty's head. He growls back, curling up in his sleeping ball. "We have dicks and can be dicks, then we chase the women out of our lives. Yet you have some secret. You can bite people, piss on them, and be just plain and simple a dick and they still love you."

"Jesus," I mutter to myself, leaping up from the couch, ignoring the growling dog. I decide to walk a few miles on Bertie's treadmill, since I found myself drunk talking to a dog, completely sober as hell.

I've been able to work myself up to two miles since Bertie's mysterious work shifts. Something was off, and Nell cemented that fact. I did what was right, and for the love of all holy, it sucks.

Everything is packed, and I'm left in sweaty clothes pacing up and down the hall on the second floor between my girls' rooms. I have several packages that will be delivered over the next few

159

days. Truly thought I'd be here when they received them. I'm wrong once again. I peer into Cody's room, knowing she'll love her new overstuffed bean bag. Shit, it's going to take up half of her room. I can picture her and Scotty curled up on it as she tells him all her woes of the day.

I force myself down to Bertie's room, leaning on the entry to it. I don't have it in me to enter. Her bedding is the same as what she had back when she entered college. I knew it damn well then and even better now. I also know it's not because Bertie was attached to the set she once purchased, but rather the fact she never took time for herself after her precious daughter entered her life and she never gave up on her hopes and dreams. Either way, the black and white bedding with pops of color will look damn good in there.

With that, I pick up my bag outside of my room and trail downstairs, waiting for the call that Jessie is outside waiting on me. Ripping a Band-Aid off an open, weeping wound has nothing on the pain I'm feeling right now. I take everything in as I pass the kitchen and finally settle on the couch. I flop down, resting my head on the back, remembering all the memories made in this house Bertie built. That's exactly what it is, hers. I don't have a spot in it until she invites me in fully. The damn woman put her job on the line for our love and continues to battle it on her own. I have to let her.

I have no idea how much time passes before I hear the familiar roar of Jessie's engine accompanied by three quick honks of the horn. I find myself chuckling and shaking my head. There's no longer a stiffness in my hip as I stand. Jessie will never know how much his old familiarity soothes away a bit of the ache. It's a piece of home or the one I used to know. I drop off the two letters on the entry table and close the door on the chapter I just lived out loud.

"Goddamn, that new hip looks damn good on you." Jessie pounds the hood of his old truck.

Max is by my side, grabbing my bag and tossing it in the bed of the truck. Don't give a shit that more than likely it's packed with snow back there or we may run into another snow storm on the way home.

"Shut the hell up." I slide into the truck. Max follows, and Jessie isn't far behind. We ride in silence for a long time before my dumbass prying friend takes it upon himself to lay into me.

"You gonna just be a puss or tell us what's going?"

A grunt is my only response.

"I see." Jessie smacks the steering wheel. "Taking the puss route. You always have. Why change now?"

I know what he's doing, and he's not very damn discreet about it. He's pushing every single one of my buttons trying to get a reaction, hoping I'll share with him. I revert back to the old Cody, gifting him with nothing but a smartass retort.

"You seem a bit too worried about pussy, Jessie. Ain't getting any at home?"

Max snorts in the backseat. Jessie's grip on the steering wheel tightens.

I don't stop there. "Revert back to the old yanking it with an old sock?"

"Fuck you," he grumbles. "I see some things never change. Wrap yourself right back up into your miserable shell for all I care."

I nod, knowing I pushed him far enough for him to shut the fuck up.

"So, you all hear Zack is projected to lead his team to state this year." Max ends his statement with a slight chuckle covering his mouth.

Oh shit, Max just ignited the fighting dynamite. Zack is dating Jessie's oldest daughter, Whit. Nobody would be good enough for his girl, and it doesn't help Zack is a player. And what I mean by a player is he's an athlete, a football quarterback, leading the rival school to breaking all records, Max's included. We all love to fling shit Jessie's way about it.

The truck comes to an abrupt stop at a gas station. "Wanna fucking walk home, boy?"

Max shakes his head, laughing his ass off as he gets out of the truck. Jessie's wide smile on his face makes me a jealous bastard. Yes, jealous. He screwed up back in the day, fought until he made it right, getting the love of his life back along with his daughter he didn't know about. Along the way, Jessie and Jules adopted Max. Jessie has it all, and I can guarantee he never pushes his friends away when they want to talk about something. He is transparent as hell, never giving up on the battle. It wasn't easy and downright ugly at points, but he came out the victor.

I will never forget the time he nearly ripped my head right off my shoulders when I got his girl, Jules, toasted on my signature drink, the Pussy Pleaser. Good damn memories… I shake my head getting out of the truck. The two-hour drive has already left me stiff. I walk around, feeling my hip ease up, then follow Jessie into the truck stop. Max is already settled in a booth, ready to eat. That boy can eat any time of the day, and just thinking of it, my stomach growls on point.

I made breakfast for the girls but couldn't stomach it myself. Also had a pork loin roast and gravy for them in the Crock-Pot. Being single as long as I have and working late nights, I've become the master of Crock-Pot recipes.

"Figured we'd eat here then make the rest of the drive," Max announces when we settle into the booth.

"Yeah, that's fine." Jessie takes off his ball cap, setting it on the booth next to him. "Should have just enough fuel to roll into town."

He grabs the mug of hot coffee that was waiting for him, drinking it down black as it was made. "You know Jules is going to make you stay with us tonight."

"My white ass." I shake my head. "I need my bed."

"Good luck with that." He chuckles. "She swears you still need someone watching after you."

"I had a damn hip replacement, not a brain transplant, for Christ's sake. I've been fine on my own for the last few weeks."

"Yeah." He smirks.

And I know I've done it again. Opened the window right open for him to try. Before he can shoot a question my way, I take it upon myself to set things straight.

"Yeah, we reconnected. She has an amazing

163

daughter around the age of Emma and Finn. She's a bit younger and amazing."

The waitress interrupts us, taking our orders.

"Hey there, guys. What can I get you?" She leans on my side of the table, nibbling on the end of her pen while staring at me. Her game is way too obvious for me.

All three of us order the chicken fried steak special. I hanker to order a beer but can't start the cycle. With the heartache I'm bearing right now, taking a step down the slippery slope to the bottom of the bottle would be way too damn easy. I settle on a Dr. Pepper.

"Anything else?" She leans down, avoiding another server rushing past her and giving me an ample view of her cleavage.

"No," I growl, hoping like hell she gets the damn hint.

She tucks tail and darts for the kitchen. Max erupts in laughter.

"Damn, you still got it, man."

I toss the salt shaker at his head. He's too fast, catching it before it pelts him between the eyes. There's a shower of salt. Once the salt is brushed off the table, I finish my story, knowing damn well Jessie won't give up until I do.

"Her name is Cody." The men's jaws are slack in shock. But I keep going. "Her dad was killed in a car accident when she was a newborn. Bertie put herself through medical school and settled here with Nell."

"Who's Nell?" Max asks, trying to keep up.

"Nell." Jessie points his finger. "Wasn't that her roommate her freshman year of college?"

I nod then take a long gulp of the cold Dr. Pepper the waitress set down. "Sure is, and let me tell you she's not my biggest fan."

I fill Jessie in on the real story of what happened back then, how I was minutes away from going all the way with Bethany. There's not one evidence of judgment as I explain all of it.

"When I got here, she was engaged to a fellow surgeon."

"Engaged!" Jessie drops back in the booth, shaking his head from side to side in shock.

"Yeah, that's what I thought." I leave out the nasty moment before my surgery. "Long story straight, Garrett ended up being a major douche, and she broke up with him. Found out from Nell after she chewed my ass that Garrett, who happens to be the chief of surgery, went to the Board and had Bertie suspended from practicing for now. I don't have many other details besides the fact he's taken away the job she loves for the time being. I don't know what else he's holding over her head."

"Why did Nell chew your ass?" Max asks.

"Long story straight."

I don't miss Jessie rolling his eyes but keeping quiet.

"I didn't give Bertie a choice last time. I left her. I walked away. Nell made it clear that now it's Bertie's choice and that I needed to give that to her."

The waitress sets down our plates of food then snags our cups for refills. She doesn't take it upon herself to flirt this time. Message received.

"Does Bertie agree with this?" Jessie asks, slicing into his chicken fried steak.

"No idea." I shrug, drenching everything with ketchup then salt and pepper.

"You're a dumbass, Cody Sterling, truly a dumbass," he grunts, shoving food in his mouth and talking around it. "You finally get the girl back and then walk away. I truly didn't think you could get any dumber than you already were."

Slicing into my food, I glare him down. "I didn't just walk out on her this time. She damn well knows where I stand and that I want her and her daughter in my life, whether it's at her house or back at mine."

"What did she say when you told her this?" Max asks with his plate already clean.

"Jesus." I slam my fork down my plate. "You two are worse than two old biddies gossiping at the senior center."

"Well?" Max leans back, eyeing Jessie's food.

"Nothing. She heard me and didn't say much of anything." I fork up a heap of steak and potatoes, bringing them to my mouth. "Now this discussion is closed. No more fucking questions."

The assholes let me finish my meal in silence. Max polished off both Jessie's and my plate without asking. Then ordered a damn dessert. Lord, help the kid if his metabolism ever catches up to him. It won't be a pretty sight.

"I'll get the bill." Jessie places his hat back on his head.

"No." I scoot out of the booth, standing tall. Little to no ache to be felt. "It's enough you brought me here and picked me up. Not to mention visited me all those times in the hospital."

"Thanks, man. And ya, how about not going and

try dying on us again."

I shake my head, pretty damn sure I won't live that one day down anytime soon. Now that I'm out of the woods, I'm sure I'll be catching shit for it for years to come.

"Yeah, I thought you'd be using a walker or some shit, old man," Max adds.

He may be younger, faster, and stronger, but he doesn't see the punch to his shoulder coming. He yelps, rubbing out the pain as I stride to the counter. I pluck a toothpick from the dispenser while waiting on the cashier. This place is hopping, and I'm sure it's because of their food. For a greasy truck stop, it is damn good. When it's my turn, I hand the older gal my bill, perch the toothpick between my lips, and pull my wallet from my back pocket.

I'm generous, leaving a ten-dollar tip for the over-eager waitress. Would've been way less if she never got the hint, that's for damn sure. Max and Jessie are still deep in conversation at the table while Max works on his dessert. I decide to grab a bottle of water and a large bag of seeds at the convenience store attached to the restaurant. I'll need something to do with my nervous energy over the next three hours.

If I thought the restaurant was busy and crowded, I was wrong. There are people everywhere in here. I find dill pickle sunflower seeds fast enough and just snag a bottle of water, not looking at the price or brand. Jesus, every line is about six people deep. My frustration grows even though they are moving fast enough.

"Daddy." A sweet little voice gets my attention.

A tiny blonde girl. Her hair isn't curly, but damn

it, I'm taken back to the little one I know with wild curly hair.

"Can I get this?" She holds up a bag of barbecue potato chips, waving them high. "Please, please, please. I will be so good for the rest of the drive. I swear I won't ask how much longer again."

The dad grunts, adjusting all the road trip snacks in his hands. She beams wildly, joining his side in the line right next to me. The tiny one begins to hum then strings together words.

"Lime and coconut. Lime, coconut. Put 'em together."

Her dad chuckles and helps her with the words of the song, "Put the lime in the coconut."

They sing it a few times before I check out. The song gets caught in my head, and I find myself humming it as I walk out to the truck. Jessie and Max lean on the sides, chatting it up. I catch another glimpse of bright blonde hair.

The girl skips across the parking lot with her bag of treasures clutched to her chest. Her dad hollers at her then drops the bags in his hand. I'm closer to her, letting my own purchases fall to the ground and dart for her. A bright red sports car zooms through the parking lot. She doesn't see it nor does the driver see her.

I lurch forward, snagging the back of her sweater, tugging with all my might until I can get my other hand on her. We both topple back. The harsh cement welcomes my back with a thud, knocking all the air from my lungs. I keep her tucked to my chest, not wanting the pavement to harm her in any way.

"Robbie!" Her dad races up to us. "Robbie, are

you okay?"

The little one in my arms squirms until she's free and runs to her father. I hear yelling, looking to my side to see Jessie ripping the driver's ass. Max is on standby in case he needs to pull Jessie back.

"Daddy." She shoots her arms in the air. "Daddy."

She tucks her head in the crook of his neck while she sobs.

"You're okay, sweetie, you're okay." He pats her back.

I feel as if I'm interrupting an intimate moment, so I bend over and pluck my bag from the ground and start for the truck.

"Hey."

I turn to the voice to see the dad stepping toward me.

"Thank you." He shakes his head. "Jesus, thank you. I wouldn't have…"

I raise a hand, waving him off. "No worries, man. I'm glad she's safe."

"Thank you," he says again.

I turn to walk back to the truck, but he's not done.

"If I ever lost her, I wouldn't be able to go on. She's my world."

I rake my hand through my hair. "I get it. I really get it."

Then a bright flash of yellow catches my attention. Looking closer, I see the little girl is wearing a pair of canary yellow boots just like Cody's. I smile wide and wave to them one more final time. As I stride to the truck, I find myself singing "Put the Lime in the Coconut."

None of it's lost on me.

Jessie slams the truck door, still seething from the careless driver. He pounds the steering wheel. "Some young dumb kid. He has no fucking idea he nearly killed a child and didn't seem to give two shits."

"Calm down, Dad." Max pats his shoulder from the back. "Pretty sure you left him with piss-soaked, overpriced designer jeans."

Jessie shakes his head. "You just never know and can't take anything for granted. Life is too damn short for careless actions like that. Should've smashed the little puke's face in."

With that, Jessie pulls the truck out on the highway. I stare out the window, watching the mile markers tick by. Road signs of every color blur past as does the scenery. A bright yellow one catches my attention. With the sight of that color, my future is planned. Fuck letting her make a choice and fighting her own fight. Fuck that.

"Turn around," I bark out.

Jessie startles behind the wheel, glancing over at me.

I slam the dash of his truck with my fist. "Turn the fuck around right now. I'm not leaving them."

Chapter 17

Bertie

"Mom, he said we will still be best friends and he's sending us stuff in the mail." Cody kicks her legs in the backseat from her booster seat. All I really see is a bright flash of yellow.

"And he's coming back three times every month and showed me how to FaceTime him, so I get to see Junior every single day."

"That's great, honey." My eyes sting and swell with the need to cry and sob, but I keep them back.

"You love him, huh?"

I glance in the rearview mirror to see her tilting her head, staring at me.

"What?" I ask.

"You love him, Mom. I know you do."

There's no use lying to her. She's smarter than any of us could ever realize. "I do love him."

"Then why didn't you tell him to stay? He would've stayed. He loves babysitting Richard

Noggin."

I chuckle and shake my head. "That's the complicated part, sweetie.

"But why?"

I bring my car to a stop at a red light and glance back at her. "I don't know how to explain it, but just know Cody will come back."

She interrupts me. "You mean Junior."

I nod and smile. "Yes, I mean Junior. He will be in our lives forever. Just right now, the time isn't exactly perfect."

"Oh." She smacks her lips together. "Like when I want to go to the Jump Time and your feet hurt and you're not nice. Like that?"

The light turns green. "Yeah, baby, just like that."

"Okay." She's silent for a few blocks. "Hey, Mom."

"Yeah?"

"Can we get Scotty a girlfriend?"

The school comes into sight. "What?"

I glance up to her in the rearview mirror. She has her hands clasped together over her chest.

"Please, please, please."

"Scotty doesn't need a girlfriend." I pull into the long lane for parent drop off and make eye contact with her in the mirror.

"Yes, he does," she replies.

"No, he doesn't." I shake my head. Not going to ensue an argument with my little girl first thing in the morning.

"Yeah, he does." She nods her head.

I glance forward to see the line hasn't moved an inch. "Okay, Cody, tell me why you think Scotty needs a girlfriend."

"Junior said that if he had a girlfriend and was getting some, he wouldn't be so mean and grumpy." She beams proudly with her reasoning.

I burst out in laughter. I should not be laughing. It's not funny, and I can't believe those words just came out of my little girl's mouth. But I can picture Scotty nipping at Cody or hiking his leg to piss on his pant leg, and then I laugh even damn harder at the whole scene.

"What's so funny, Mom? He needs a girlfriend and then he'll be a nice dog." She brushes her hair back. "A girl in my class takes her dog to 4-H, and if I can get Scotty nice, I know he'll win."

I wipe the happy tears away and nod. "I agree, sweetie, Scotty needs a girlfriend, but," I hold up my finger, "we will need to do our research before we get him one."

"Yes." She throws her arm up in the air as I creep up in the drop-off lane. "I'm going to tell everyone that my dog will win. I just know he will."

"Hey, now." I glance back over my shoulder. "Be humble. Don't brag. You'll need to work hard with Scotty, okay?"

She nods. "Okay, Mom, I'll try. Junior told me I need to walk and talk like a boss."

Oh hell. I swear he's gifted this girl with years of confidence, something I never thought I'd see, and he did it in a month or so. And I let him go. I don't have time to think about it as we pull right up in front of the school, the witchy guard watching us with a death glare.

I'm not supposed to hop out of the car and hug

and kiss her, but I do every morning. I also get a monthly notice that I'm breaking school protocol. I toss them in the trash every single time. They can kiss my ass. I will never miss a chance to hug and kiss on my most prized gift. She's my world.

Cody hops out of the back of the car, adjusting her backpack and wiggling her pants up her hips. I kneel before her, holding my arms wide open.

"Come here, my sweet, brave girl."

Cody shakes her head then leaps into my chest. "Mom, I'm a warrior. Junior told me so."

I run my hand up and down her back. "Yes, you are."

I'd do anything for this girl; I hug her extra long today.

"'Kay, Mom, have to go to Learning Club, okay?" She wiggles out of my squeeze.

"Okay." I nod and stand up. "I'll pick you up after school today, okay? We are going out for pizza with Aunt Nell then to Jump Time."

Cody jumps up and down. "Best day ever."

And with that, she darts off into the school. Man, only to have that zest and innocence for life again. It's priceless, and when we are in that stage, we have no idea we have the greatest gift. I square my shoulders and set off to do way too adult-y shit today.

There's not much traffic as I drive across town to my lawyer's office. Once I'm parked, I pick up my cell phone. I have his number. I run my finger over his contact, admiring his contact picture. The two loves of my world smiling back at me with the devil dog sitting right between them.

"Cody, why did I send you away?" I whisper to

the phone. "If I'm being honest, I need you more than anything right now."

I admire his disheveled hair and scruff on his jawline. It's all sexiness. The man turns heads everywhere he goes. But it's so much more than that. It's the love, kindness, and raw vulnerability. I tuck my phone away, knowing I could stare at it all day while talking myself out of calling Cody.

"Ms. Cooper, we're ready for you." A receptionist leads me back to a conference room, where my lawyer relaxes in an overstuffed leather chair.

"Bertie, come on in." He waves his hand, his smile never faltering.

Unease creeps up my spine. I'm not sure how to feel about his happiness. I know it's more than likely favoring me, but it still creeps me out at the same time.

"I have good news." He flips open the lid of his MacBook. "Excuse me. Would you like water or coffee?"

I shake my head. "No, thanks. I'm good."

"Well, first off, I shouldn't be this energized considering I haven't slept since you left my office."

"You what?" I cough out.

"You heard me right. That list you offered was pure gold."

"The list." Even though I understand everything he says, I find myself repeating myself. Chalk it up to shock.

"Yes. I interviewed several hospital employees and found out way more than I ever bargained for." He turns his MacBook my way. Image after image of bruises, cuts, and sex photos come into view. "This is why he was scrambling."

My hand goes to my throat as I gasp. "What is this?"

"This is what Garrett does. Seems he's been doing it for years. My phone has been ringing off the hook with women from his college years. Some of the nurses told me names that Garrett threatened them with. He encouraged the women to look up what happened to them. The man is pure evil."

"But—bu—but he never hurt me."

"Not yet." McDouglas nods. "Garrett found himself in quite a bit of trouble his first year of residency. Seems his parents did quite the job of cleaning up the mess, but it seems he didn't learn his lesson. His parents have paid off more people than you can imagine."

"Okay." I nod.

"This time they told him to get married or he was cut off. They're tired and honestly more than likely financially exhausted. He'd be in prison if it weren't for their help, and they will write him off if he doesn't get married and settled down."

"But that doesn't help him," I say.

"No, it doesn't, but I'm guessing they're desperate and were reaching for straws."

The puzzle pieces click into place one by one. My stomach roils low in my belly, the stinging sensation of bile creeping up my throat. I manage to talk through it all. "So, he found me. A single mom with a young child and a reputable past to be his key to righting all of his wrongs."

"Yes, Bertie, that's exactly what he did." He reaches over, covering my hand with his. It reminds me of way a loving grandpa would do to his favorite grandkid. "All I need is a yes, and the hospital board and local authorities will have all of this information within the hour."

This isn't something easy to decide on. We aren't talking what kind of cheese you want on your hamburger. No, it's so much worse. My courageous girl comes to mind. I'd always want her to fight for what's right, no matter how scary it is.

"Do it." I stand up, straightening out my shirt and jerking my chin.

"On it." He leaps up from his chair. "Stay home for the next few days until he's in custody. I'm going to warn you, Bertie, it's going to get ugly. Damn ugly."

"There's always ugly before the beauty." I walk out of his office with trembling hands.

I sit in my car for minutes, hell, who knows, hours…recalling everything about Garrett. There was a nasty nurse before me, and he gave me every excuse in the book. I bought all his bullshit. Then there was Brittany, who was my really good friend. We'd always bring each other leftovers, and she even hung out with me and my daughter a handful of times, but Garrett taunted me with that as well. Told me she came onto him. Lies. All lies.

My brain reels with all the sneaky shit he did. The more I think about it, the more pissed off I get that I was hook, line, and sinker for the asshole. He played a damn good game, and I was his pawn. A pawn that had no chance in hell to survive. He picked the wrong girl this time. The joke will be on him. I would be a liar if I said I wasn't scared. I'm frightened beyond belief.

Without thinking, I dial Cody's number. It goes straight to voicemail, but it doesn't stop me from listening to his warm comforting voice.

"Cody, it's Junior. If I don't answer, I'm slinging drinks at my bar or in the bathroom. Love you, little squirt, and will call you right back."

I lose it. The tears blind me to the point I can't see a damn thing. My body shakes and vibrates as I realize my biggest mistake. Yes, he screwed up, but I ruined it all shoving him out the door.

I find another contact on my phone and hit send. She answers on the first ring.

"Hey."

"Nell," I sob out. "I need you."

After sending her my location, I continue to cry and shake until she arrives. I'm not sure how I manage it, but I find myself in her car staring out the window at the passing scenery. Nell doesn't speak a word or even ask a question.

"Tacos," I mumble. "We need tacos. Lots and lots of them."

She whips into the nearest Taco Time, ordering a shit ton of tacos, making sure we get extra ranch and green sauce. I never let her pay for shit. But today is a different story. She pulls up to my house, grabs the tacos, then helps me out of the car. Scotty yaps at us when we enter. I go straight for the couch, cuddling up to the end of it.

"Wine or vodka?" Nell shouts from the kitchen.

"Neither. I need tacos and you," I holler back.

Nell enters with the bag of tacos. I uncurl from the couch, going to town on the tacos. Nell doesn't ask what in the hell is going on until I'm ready to offer it up. I swear the longer I let myself think on it, the more everything makes sense. I'm such a damn fool.

Once I gain my bearings for the briefest of moments, I spill everything to Nell. She doesn't say a word as I ramble on and on, berating my idiot self.

"And if you say I told you so, I swear to God I will never talk to you again. I won't even look at you. I'll forget your name and put some kind of spell on you."

Nell drops her taco raising up both of her hands. "Chill, lady. I got you. I'm here for you. Haven't left your side so far and not about to. We will take Cody out to pizza tonight and to Jump Town or whatever in the hell it's called. Then we will come home, tuck her in, take a bottle of wine to bed, and be just fine while that asshole is getting locked up."

"You promise?" Tears strike again. Jesus, I'm way too emotional, but I don't have anything to compare this to.

"I promise." She picks her taco back up. "Now quit crying. You leak weak."

I toss my wrapper at her, the tears falling faster with laughter mixed in. I relax back on the couch, tugging a blanket over me. I'm so damn tired.

"Wake me up at ten minutes before we need to go."

"Got it, boss." Nell flicks on the television. I remain awake long enough to see her open her laptop. That's the silver lining about having friends who work from home. They are there for you any time of the day.

***

Only to be napping on the couch right now. The shrill screams of children and the pizza not settling well in my stomach are about to make me cry, even though my tears dried up a long time ago.

"Mom, watch us. Mom!"

"Bertie!"

I glance into the trampoline cage to see Cody and Nell bouncing up and down. Once they have my attention, they count off on their fingers then do some silly dance similar to their handshake. Then they bounce apart and do cartwheels in opposite directions. Well, Nell does cartwheels. Cody barely manages not to knock herself out with her kneecaps. But it doesn't stop her from springing her arms up in the air and smiling.

I shoot them a thumb's up, and soon enough I'm coaxed up on the trampoline. They put me in the routine, not giving away the secret of their handshake. We wiggle our butts and do some other things then spring into cartwheels. I shock myself when I nail one, unlike Nell who does three or four in a row, same as Cody who does her own version. I fall on my ass laughing. I don't get a moment of silence or a chance to catch my breath as Nell bounds near me, jumping as hard as she can and springing me into action. Cody tackles me while we bound up and down. It exhilarates me, reminding me of all the rights in the world.

I'm light and carefree, loving life with everything I have in it. I'm going to be okay. An hour later, I'm forced to drag Cody then Nell off the damn trampolines, ready to get home and in bed. It's been one hell of a day.

Cody passes out within seconds of being tucked into her seat. Nell sings to some song on the radio as I let my head relax on the headrest. It's a glimpse of my life before he came back in. This was how it always was. But now I know there can be so much more, and I'm hungry for it.

"Hey, I gotta run home and grab some things. Want me to do it now or drop you guys off first?" Nell asks, turning down the radio.

"Take me home. I swear if you drive any longer, I'll pass out and never wake up!"

"Okay, okay, princess." She takes a right into my neighborhood.

Nell punches in the security code to my garage door. It rises, and I go to the backseat, plucking Cody from her booster seat. She doesn't stir; she's passed out cold as I walk into the garage.

"Need anything?" Nell asks. "Chocolate, condoms, cucumbers?"

"Get the hell out of here and hurry back." I shake my head, keeping Cody still on my shoulder and twisting the doorknob that leads into the kitchen.

I flick on the light to see empty taco wrappers overflowing from the trash can.

"Scotty, it's just us. Please don't bark. Your girl is out," I whisper with no response from him.

It must've been all the pieces of hamburger Nell fed him. I swear she's either a soft-hearted person or the biggest wuss I know. Every time Scotty growls at her, she gives him a pinch of food.

I make my way up the stairs, pissed I didn't drop

my purse on the counter where I always do. I put it there so I know where it is when I'm in a hurry to get out the door. I manage to lay Cody down in her bed, pulling off her boots, and tugging the blankets up over her shoulders. I drop my purse on the floor and head to the shower.

Not going to lie. It's killing me not to shower down Cody after being in that germ-infested playground, but I know waking her up would be like poking a sleeping bear with a stick. I strip down, relaxing under the hot shower. I'm so damn exhausted it's not even funny.

I let the warmth of the shower wrap me up in a relaxing hug, wringing out the remnants of silky conditioner. Once it's gone, I remain under the spray until it cools. Drying off is a challenge with my muscles relaxed and unwilling to give anymore. I pull on the first yoga pants I spot and then snag a t-shirt close to it.

It's not until I have it on that I realize it's Cody's t-shirt. The one from high school that still fits him, even if it hugged every one of his chest muscles. That damn logo on the front and his scent takes me back years, and I know everything will be okay. I toss the towel in the hamper then decide to find Scotty to see how much he's puked all over the place. I glance up to the dim lit hallway and leap back.

"Well, hello, Roberta."

"Wh—hat are you doing here?" I leap back.

"I came for what is mine." The look in Garrett's eyes is manic. His greasy hair stands on end with black smudge marks covering the white of his dress shirt. "Figured you were ready to put on your wedding ring."

"Leave now," I demand, backing up, scrambling to grasp onto something. "Get out now!"

My scream echoes around the walls. But it's his deep, roaring laughter that overpowers me. He doesn't leave; instead, he walks toward me with evil coating his every being.

"I have your ring, Roberta." He tugs out a black box from his pocket. "It's about time you put it on."

My hand wraps around the base of the lamp, but before I have the chance to fully grasp it, Garrett pounces. My breath whooshes through my lungs as my spine cracks back on the nightstand then to the floor. He doesn't stop there. His fists come into vision raining down on me. I scream each time. Fighting and struggling to be louder and louder with each blow.

"Put the ring on, bitch!" One final blow makes everything go black. My screams weren't loud enough.

Chapter 18

Cody

"Are you fucking kidding me?" I beat the dash.

"Take it easy, man. This is a new truck since Whit is driving my old one. You're about to beat it to hell."

I snag my dead phone from my back pocket. My girl drained it trying FaceTime out and checking out every single one of my apps. Didn't think about charging it this morning and have to plug it into Jessie's charger, then flop back in my seat. "No way a freaking wreck would stop the highway for four hours. Four fucking hours and we still have an hour and a half to go."

"Shut up and sit back," Jessie barks. "You have no idea how close I am to turning this around and going back home."

"Try it," I seethe at him.

"I'll knock you out with one punch," Max pipes up, "if you don't get your shit together."

I have no other choice but to relax and regret

every single damn second of leaving my girls. What a freaking idiot. Yeah, Bertie has options, but from this point on, I'll be involved in every single second of them. I just witnessed a little girl nearly being run over with all the life taken from her. This shit's over. Game over. I'm in her life, and if she doesn't like the choice I make, she can kiss my ass, and then I'll make her coffee.

An hour out. Clear highways. Jessie is pushing the speed limit. Thirty minutes out. Jessie still pushing the speed limit. Twenty minutes out and my cell phone goes off. A shrilling ring lights up the cab of the truck, cutting through the thick silence. I'm no fool and have felt the frustrations of my friends with each mile that has passed by.

By the time I grab my phone, the call has ended. Reaching under the seat to where it slid, I finally find it, barely managing to wrap my fingers around it. It takes all my flexibility and strength to bring it up to my face.

Missed Call: Bertie.

I squeeze the phone so damn tight it slips right back down on the floorboards.

"Are you fucking kidding me?" I roar.

I do the same thing, grabbing for the phone. It begins ringing before I have the chance to redial her number. It's a FaceTime call. I press the green button before thinking twice. There's some weird nose then complete darkness.

"Cody?" I ask.

Darkness. No bright blonde curls on display.

Nobody responds.

"Cody, are you there?"

Again, nothing but blackness. A scream fills the background.

"Get out!"

"Stop."

"Garrett. No!"

The sound of Bertie fighting for her life echoes around the cab since she's on speakerphone.

"Cody, are you there?"

"Yes." A slight whisper comes through the end of the phone.

"Where are you?" I whisper.

"Under my blankets."

"Good girl." I glance over to Jessie, giving him a nod. He picks up on it, pushing the limits of speed.

"Where's Scotty?"

"I-I-uh, don't know."

"Probably sleeping." My words are cut off with another scream of horror. "You stay right where you are."

"Junior."

"I'm coming. I'm only a few minutes away." I glare at Jessie again, urging him to run red lights or whatever the hell he has to do.

"You went home. Momma needs help."

"She does, and I swear I'm coming." I pause, gripping my forehead. "Cody, please, please do not leave where you are."

"I'm scared."

"I know, baby girl. I'm almost there."

"You promise?"

"Double pinky promise with sprinkles on top."

186

"He's hurting Mommy."

I shoot straight up in my seat. "I see your house. I'm here."

"You are." Her voice peps up.

"Yes, but." I raise my voice into a stern tone. "Cody, don't you dare come out of your blankets, do you hear me? If you hear my voice, you stay put. Don't you dare move."

"O-Okay, but how will I know?"

"I'll slide a yellow marker under the door."

"Okay, Junior."

"Cody, I'm giving my phone to my friend Max, okay? Don't you dare hang up. You talk to him. Remember Finn that I told you about?"

"Yeah. He's weird like me."

"He is. And this is his dad. He'll talk to you. I'm going to save your mom."

Max grabs the phone after ending his call with 911. Jessie brings the truck to an abrupt stop in the driveway. He killed the headlights when he pulled in. It devastated me giving the phone to Max. I'd give anything to be Cody's lifeline, but with her shrilling cries, I have no choice.

The garage door is open with the light illuminating out. Then I see it: blood, pools and pools of it. Nell lies unconscious on the ground. Jessie stays back, tending to her while I burst into the house. There's an eerie silence that coats the hollows of the house. Scotty doesn't even make a peep.

I take the steps two at a time. A dull glow comes from Cody's room. She's listened to me, remaining tucked under blankets talking to Max. Her sweet little whispers float out into the hall. She's safe. I move on. It's what I see next that turns my blood ice cold.

Bertie, beaten and shattered, is sprawled out on her bed. She's like a starfish, strung out taut. Her blonde hair is no longer recognizable, her features a thing of the past. I remain still, shock taking over my body. Her lamp lies on the carpet, broken and the glass shattered.

"Hey, baby, that ring looks great." Garrett strides out of her bathroom, rolling up his sleeves. "We can tell my parents you were in an accident. I know how to wreck a car without the police looking into it." He nears the bed. "Oh, and we can tell the authorities your lawyer was some cheap bastard looking to take down a Chief of Surgery to make a quick buck."

He leans down, brushing back her hair. It takes everything inside me not to leap into action and beat the life out of the fuck.

"I'll always be here for you, Roberta." He kisses her lifeless forehead. "We can buy that daughter of yours a new dog, too."

Garrett settles on the bed, giving me his backside while he whispers fucked-up promises to Bertie. I wait seven, eight, nine seconds before making a move. If he sees me coming, who knows what he'd do to Bertie?

I've never known what self-constraint was until now. Everything before was child's play. I don't give a shit if he sees me or not. That mother-fucker's hands don't deserve the grace of her skin. The enchanted, self-centered son of a bitch doesn't even pick up on my footsteps tromping on the plush carpet towards him. It's when my boot squishes in crimson blood that I see red.

I don't think. I don't care about anyone but the primary goal of killing Garrett. That bastard will flatline under my own hands. I clock the bastard in the back of the head. My knuckles creak and crack when they collide with the base of his skull.

It's enough to knock him off the bed. I pounce on him, throttling the hell out of his face until he's limp, but it's not enough. My hands wrap around his neck, squeezing until I don't feel anything below them.

"Cody," a whisper comes.

I swear it's my imagination.

"Junior, please." It's softer this time. "I need you."

I glance up, squeezing tighter on the motherfucker's throat, to see Bertie staring at me, pleading with her gaze.

"Cody needs you." Her hand flops to the side.

I leap up into action, making sure to stomp on Garrett's chest and throttle him in the ribs with my boots. I grab her in my arms, cradling her to my chest.

"Junior."

I look up to see Bertie's mini-me staring at me with a frightened stare.

"Just a minute, baby girl. Hang up on Max and call 911."

I scoop Bertie up in my arms. Her body is heavy and utterly lifeless. My knees weaken at once, but I carry on for the little girl in the middle of the hall.

"Go downstairs. Get out to the garage, baby girl. I'm right behind. So is your mommy."

She follows my instructions, racing down the

steps and out into the garage. Cody trips on the first step, but I see it. Scotty's bloody body next to Nell's. Jessie sees us, doing his best to cover it all up.

"Daddy!" Cody's voice screams. "Daddy, I'm so scared."

Max grabs Bertie from my arms. Parts of me want to punch him straight in the face, and the others are thankful.

"Come here." I open my arms to Cody. She races into them, burying her face in the crook of my neck.

"I got you, baby girl." I run my hand up and down her back. "I got you."

She sobs and wails in my arms. Her tiny feet are kicking against my stomach. "I'm so scareded, Dad."

"I know. I have you, sweet girl." I continue to run my hand up and down her back, knowing the trauma she's gone through has been hell and she's talking to the picture frame near her bed.

"Jun—Dad, please help me."

Her words stun the shit out of me. I remain quiet for a few ticks and then speak, clutching her tighter to me. "I'm not letting you go, Cody. I won't let you go."

"Mom was so bloody."

Red and blue lights serenade the inside of the garage. "Yes, she was." I rub my hand faster up and down her back. "But I hear your crazy uncle Trent is working. He'll take real good care of your mom."

"Where's Scotty?" she cries out.

I don't have a chance to answer her before the cops are yelling in our faces. It's Max who comes to the rescue, telling them exactly where Garrett is. The rest is a blur. All I do know is that I keep my sweet little girl in my arms tucked against my chest until we get word on her mom and my future wife.

Chapter 19

Cody

There was so much damn blood. I can't get over the horror scene I walked into. Closing my eyes, relaxed back on the waiting room chair, it's all I still see, even with sweet Cody cuddled against my chest and asleep. Minutes feel like hours and hours like an eternity as we wait and wait. Max and Jessie forced me to quit pacing a while ago.

Nell is being treated for a concussion and getting some stitches. She ended up with a nasty head wound, hence all the blood.

"Max, can you take her? I'm going to check in again."

He nods, taking Cody from my arms and settling down onto a worn leather couch.

"I'm coming with you," Jessie adds. "We don't need your temper flaring up. It won't get you anywhere."

I nod, not giving a shit what he says or anyone else

for that fact. She has to be okay. She just has to be. I pace the hallway outside the ER until I spot a nurse.

"Excuse me, is there any word on Bertie Cooper?" I'm quick to correct myself. "I mean Roberta Cooper."

"Are you family?" she asks.

I stall, knowing it's going to take a lie here. More than likely, this nurse knows Bertie from working at the same hospital. She's an only child. I'm not sure how public Bertie has made that fact.

"I'm her brother." I run my hands through my hair. "Got here as fast as I could. Can I see her please?"

"And you are?" She points to Jessie.

"Just a friend of his." He hitches me a thumb towards me. "Here for moral support."

"Okay, give me a few minutes to go check. Wait here, and you won't be able to go back just yet." She points at Jessie.

"Thank you." I clasp my hands on top of my head in relief.

"Cody, you need to keep your cool." Jessie slaps a hand on my shoulder. "You don't need to go getting upset and losing your shit at the sight of Bertie. The cops will be here anytime to question you."

I nod, continuing to wear holes in the tile.

"The last thing Bertie and Cody need is your ass behind bars."

"I was protecting her," I grit out.

"I know that. You know that. And she knows that, man. But you really fucked him up, so you'll really need to keep your cool when they interview you. Keep all emotions out of it and stick to the facts."

I nod, knowing he's right. "I will. I'm not going to do anything to jeopardize being away from my girls."

"Sir." The same nurse pokes her head out from behind a door. "You can come back."

Jessie squeezes my shoulder. "Keep your cool and be strong for her."

I don't reply, following the nurse, balling and unballing my fist and then shaking out my fingers. I never wanted to smell the stale, putrid aroma of a hospital again. But here I am, breathing it in.

"She's been through quite a lot of trauma. She's awake, but if we can't get her to settle down, then she'll have to be sedated. She keeps calling for a Cody." I burst past the nurse, striding to Bertie's bedside.

"Baby, I'm here."

Her head whips to the side. At the sound of my voice, she erupts into uncontrollable tears.

"Hey, hey, none of that." I kiss the top of her head. "I'm here."

She struggles to get words out but can't through her hiccupping sobs.

"Sssshhhh, baby, listen. Cody is fine, Nell is fine. Everything is all good." I kiss the top of her head. God, I want her lips, but they're cracked and swollen. Her face has been beaten so badly she's unrecognizable.

"Garr—" She points to her face. "Did."

"Sssshh." I nod, agreeing with her. "He's in custody."

Which isn't a full lie, but I did leave out that he's also here in this hospital in far worse shape than she is. Jessie is right; I'm going to have to play my cards smart when I'm interviewed.

"Cody," she stutters out.

"She's out in the waiting room with Max and Jessie. Nell is getting stitches. Everyone is just fine," I repeat over and over, hoping to offer her some comfort.

"Jules." She pauses, gulping down, her dry lips sticking to each other. "Want her to take care of Cody."

"Yeah, baby, she's on her way up. We are all here for you."

I catch sight of a nurse walking by. "Hey, excuse me?"

Moments later, the curtain is pulled back by the same nurse. "Yes?"

"Can she have some ice chips or something?"

"Just a moment. I'll be right back." She disappears behind the curtain.

It's a good thing Bertie is still in the ER and not rushed into surgery. That's what I keep telling myself over and over. It doesn't take away the fact she's so beaten it brings me to my knees. The nurse returns with the ice with strict instructions to not to overdo it.

"Now." Bertie struggles to raise an arm.

"Okay, just one, baby." I dig the smallest one from the cup, placing it between her lips, making sure to wet her lips.

"I love you, Cody," she whispers, moving the ice cube around in her mouth.

"Don't talk, baby." I want more than anything to cup her cheeks. "Everything is fine."

Once the ice cube melts in her mouth, she speaks. "I want to go home."

I hold my wince inside, feeling it tug on my insides. I don't dare to tell her. Scotty didn't make it. He fought the battle until Nell showed up. Tears build up in my eyes thinking about my old buddy.

"Okay, baby, you need to rest here, and then I'll take you to your house." I mentally calculate all the manpower I have on my side. My family will pull through. They're not blood but so much more. They'll clean up the mess. "You just need to rest, baby."

"No." She manages to reach up and squeeze my wrist. "No, I want to go home with you, back to your place."

"You do?" Jesus, it takes everything inside of me to not devour her lips.

"My home is where you are, Cody Sterling. It always has been."

I give her another ice cube as she coughs over her words. I give her seconds to let it melt against her tongue.

"I always knew it was where I belonged," she whispers, with her eyelids fluttering shut.

As much as it pains me to leave her touch, I rush to the curtain, ripping it open and hollering for a nurse. She reassures me it's the medicine they've given her and that she'll be coming in and out.

She quirks a brow at me. "And I've never seen a brother so cozy with his sister."

I clear my throat, no way in hell ready to be kicked out of the room. "We are a close-knit family. I'm her only living sibling, and we, uh, lean on each other."

"Sure." She shakes her head. "The doctor will be a while. Whatever and however you two do things, just stay by her side. She needs you."

"Sure thing." I wink, thankful as hell she's letting me stay with Bertie.

I go back to her, lacing my fingers in hers, rocking back and forth, hoping like hell she remembers saying it and even more it's what she truly wants. Hours tick by as Bertie remains in her peaceful slumber. I check my phone every few minutes. It remained on silent, but I've found out Jules made it and has little Cody at a hotel room where she never woke from her slumber. I can't imagine the fear Cody will experience waking up in an odd place with an unfamiliar face after what she went through the past few hours.

There's no one else I'd trust besides Jules. I don't even have to remind her to FaceTime. She'll know exactly what to do. The next text message that comes through is that Nell is with Jules in the hotel suite. It lays some of my nerves to rest.

"Cody." Bertie stirs in the bed, gripping my hand.

"I'm here, baby." I keep hold of her hand, pressing my lips to the top of her head. "I'm here. Everyone is safe," I repeat over and over again.

Not long after she stirs awake, the fucking doctor finally appears. The nurse's words "it will be a while" was a complete lie. It was more like hours.

"Doctor Roberta Cooper, it's good to see you awake."

"Bertie." A dry cough splutters deep from her throat. "Don't call me Roberta."

He rubs his temples and starts over again. "Okay,

Bertie, it's nice to see you awake."

He pauses, but nobody talks, so he takes it upon himself to carry on.

"Thank you, Doctor Reid," she croaks.

Of course, she knows him. I can't imagine how uncomfortable this has to be for her. The pain she's experiencing trumps all of it.

He smiles kindly at her. "You know protocol and all I'll give you like any other patient. Due to your injuries, we are going to keep you overnight to monitor you. We've run a full blood test. We were going to proceed with X-rays, but something in your blood test came up positive, so we didn't."

I panic at his words. "Injuries" is all I pick up on and freak the shit out. I drop her hand and brawl up to my feet. "What? What did you find?"

"Calm down, sir, and let me finish."

"Bullshit," I roar. "What did you find?"

I grasp my hip on instinct even though the pain isn't there. What I'm feeling is so much worse.

"Sit."

This time, it isn't the young doctor in front of me. It's Bertie. I listen and sit with my jaw clenched and teeth grinding. A few seconds of silence floats by before the doctor begins talking.

"Your HCG levels are elevated, alerting me to the fact you may be pregnant. Are there any chances of this? We didn't want to go ahead with an x-ray."

The silence deafens me. I glance to Bertie to the doctor and back to Bertie.

"Yes, it could be possible."

"Okay." He nods, like he didn't just knock my world on its side.

He rattles on about her care and the fact she'll only be here overnight. Once he leaves, I glance over at Bertie. Her cheeks are flushed underneath the bruising. We don't speak of the news the doctor just delivered, and I'm thankful for that. I hope like hell it isn't a cruel joke.

"Take me home, Cody Sterling."

"Home?" I squeeze her hand.

"Home is wherever you are. Take me home," she whispers again, her eyes fluttering shut.

"I'll pack up your house, baby."

Chapter 20

Cody

Life is a funny joke. Cruel in intention. Taking away a mother from her daughter only because one bad seed entered the scene. I don't even give a shit that it was for a matter of hours or days. It still pisses me off. The cries and heartache that have stemmed from that day will never bring back the same man I once was.

Cody remains tethered to my side as we get through each part of the day. Her hand squeezes mine as she selects the brightest yellow flowers in the shop. She doesn't take it lightly as she plucks each one up, forming a gorgeous bouquet arraying in every shade of yellow.

Tears stream down her face as she guides me to the counter of the flower shop. I can't speak or even think or I'd be as big a mess as her.

"Dad," she glances up at me, "Mom did say he could've got a girlfriend you know?"

I drop to one knee, cupping her cheek. "He loved you, baby girl. Hell, he'd piss and bark at anyone that got near you. He went out of his way protecting you."

She nods. "His barks woke me up. I was so confused when he wasn't on my pillow, then I heard Mom's screams."

She drops the flowers, wrapping her arms around my neck. I feel each and every one of her sobs. I wait, letting her get them all out before whispering into her ear. This isn't the first time Cody has spilled her grief on me. I take it each and every time.

"He was your dog. He loved you so fiercely that he would never let anything or anyone hurt you. He tried his hardest, baby girl." I kiss the top of her head and whisper, "Baby girl, you're brilliant, talented, and the most loving girl I know."

"I know." She sniffles again then straightens up and gathers the fallen flowers on the ground. "We will give him all the flowers every day, huh, Dad?"

"We sure will." I kiss the top of her head again completely, madly in love with this girl. She's become my daughter in every way possible.

She never stopped calling me Dad from the day of the accident, and I never dared correct her or ask Bertie for permission. No one can ever take them from me. It's the greatest accomplishment of my life.

That's how every Sunday goes. Cody and I go to the flower shop, and she buys an arrangement for Scotty. Her dog. Her best friend that was killed by the evil in the world. He was doing his job. I'll never have the words to describe this to her. How can I justify an evil son of a bitch who took so much greatness from the world?

Cody signs her name on the tab with most of the letters appearing backwards. Marge, my hometown florist, smiles brightly back at her, giving her a wink. "You sure picked out pretty ones this week."

"Thank you." Cody wipes the tears from her cheeks. "My little Richard Noggin will love these."

I bite down on my bottom lip and shake my head. Marge squeezes Cody's hand, and then we are off to my house, the same home Bertie begged to come home to. We never visited the home she built with her daughter. It was left in the past like all of our prior mistakes. And the walls of my house became a home filled with love, happiness, and everything I could ever desire.

Cody loves the fact my truck is a single cab and she gets to sit in the front. The little shit even tries to get away without wearing her buckle. I bust her every single time.

"Dad." Cody bursts open the door once we pull into my drive. "I'm taking these to Scotty's grave."

"Okay, missy, I'll watch from the porch."

"It might be a while because Scotty and I have lots and lots to talk about with my new school and all."

With that, she's races off toward the headstone with flashes of yellow from her boots and flowers as if she is a shining beacon. I watch until I can barely see a speck on the horizon and know she's settled crisscross applesauce facing Scotty's headstone. Some days she'll talk to him for hours until I go and gather her, and others she dances right up the steps to our house with a smile on her face.

Her new school is homeschool with Jules as the teacher and Emma and Finn the only other students.

There were awkward times as Emma, the boss of the roost, fought to take over and Cody and Finn learned to figure out each other's quirks. In time, they gelled and are excelling in their learning. Cody's letters may be backwards, but her knowledge is endless.

I walk backward up the sidewalk, keeping my sight on her. The steps creak and crack as I walk up each one of them. I settle into my favorite rocking chair, watching my girl talk to her dog she loves with all her heart and soul. The same devil dog who saved her life.

"Hey, babe." A warm hand reaches over, covering mine.

And her mom's life.

"How's she doing?" Bertie asks, rubbing her swollen belly.

"She misses him. Her soul is broken. She cried and picked out every yellow flower they had like she always does."

"Yeah." Bertie rocks with a smirk on her face.

The slight scar on her forehead guts me every time I see it. It could've been so much worse. I'll never forget the moment she woke up and asked me to take her home. I was all-in. The only thing I didn't understand was home meant mine. My girl was finally back in my life.

The truth was revealed that night, and Garrett clung to life. I like to think it was because no one was rooting for him that later made him take the plunge to flatline. No one could save him. In all honesty and my best doctor lingo, it was a collapsed lung from a broken rib. He was gone, and I took Bertie and my girl home. That night was so chaotic, and between my story, Bertie's, Nell's, Cody's, and the pile of evidence against Garrett, the case was closed.

Bertie was expecting, and that piece of news was glorious and scary as shit. She battled for life and for the one growing inside her. Garrett took away Cody's mom for days, and for that I will never be able to forgive him. The board reinstated her license right away. She became a practicing doctor in our tiny hometown office once she had the strength. Her knowledge knew no bounds, and the townspeople welcomed her with arms wide open. They drank her in like an ice-cold glass of lemonade. She refreshes everything she touches. I'm living proof.

It was all perfect except for the tiny shatter in our family. Scotty was gone.

"You missing the office?" I ask, rocking in unison with her.

"Will you be mad if I say yes?"

I scoff. "Would be worried if you said no, doctor."

She chuckles, rubbing her belly. She's days away from popping, and Lord, I've never understood a woman pregnant and stressed out. It's been heaven and hell all at the same time. I swear pulling this woman away from her job is impossible. We can't even go to the grocery store without someone stopping her. And of course, Bertie listens and gives her best advice, most of it ending with the comment to call the office, and you can damn sure bet Bertie has followed up on each and every patient.

A yelping sound gets my attention. Bertie rocks forward, reaching down, grabbing a puppy from a box.

"Think this will help?" She smiles with a

squirming puppy in her hand. "They were giving them away at the grocery store today. Jules got one for Emma, too." She winks.

Like Jules getting a puppy also would help the situation.

"Do you know the pedigree?" I quirk an eyebrow.

"Cardboard box…" She trails off.

"Its ears are floppy, and it's the same color as Scotty."

"It's a she and Scotty's girlfriend." She pauses, even tearing up. That damn dog did us all in. "She's perfect and spoke to me."

I smile wide. "It's his girlfriend."

"Yes, he got a girlfriend."

The sound of footsteps come tromping up the stairs. Cody keeps her vision focused on her fumbling fingers.

The puppy lets out a high-pitched yelp, piercing my eardrums.

This coaxes Cody out of her trance. Her messy blonde curls bound up. It takes her only a matter of seconds before she puts the puzzle pieces together. Her tentative smile fades into a frown. No one will ever replace Scotty. It's not until the naughty pup nips at Bertie's hands that Cody smiles wide and races up the sidewalk and porch steps.

"Oh my God. Oh my God." She drops to her knees before her mom. "What is this?"

"Your new best friend," Bertie replies.

I can tell by the coarse hair of the dog and floppy ears that this puppy will be far worse than Scotty ever dared being. Talk about reincarnation on steroids.

"It's mine?" She slaps her chest in question.

The dog yips and scrambles in Bertie's hands. It's not until Cody pulls the pup to her chest that it settles down. And I swear to God, shock me down to death, somehow Scotty's evil glare shines back at me.

"Are you a boy or girl?" Cody flips the pup over. "Oh, you're a girl. You're Scotty's girlfriend. Your name is Sasha. He always wanted a Sasha."

Cody bursts into the house, leaving Bertie and me on the porch. We rock back and forth on our rockers. We've been through it all and have so much more to look forward to.

"I thought Cody Junior would be a nice name."

"There's too many damn Codys and a Junior around here." Bertie continues to rub her rounded belly while squeezing my hand.

"Claude?" I squeeze her hand right back. "That's a solid and sturdy name."

"No."

"A hard no?" I ask.

"Hard as hell, and did you miss the fact she has already named the dog?" She continues to rock back and forth.

I decide to go for it all. Hell, it's the motto of my life now. I'll never walk away or back down because of past sins.

"I'm talking baby names. We know it's another girl." Yes, God played his hand real damn well giving the playboy two girls. "Robby."

"Robby," Bertie repeats.

I remain silent, having no idea where she'd be on this.

"Robby," she repeats again. "I like it."

Internally I fist pump but end up coughing. I grasp

206

my chest, hacking up the best cough I can muster.

"Are you getting sick?" Bertie leans forward in the rocker with her hands on her swollen belly in full doctor mode.

I cough again for good measure and wink. "I'm so sick, doc."

That only earns me a smack on the back of the head as we both gaze toward the sunset, relishing in the miracle of us.

Epilogue

Cody

I rock back and forth, watching the kids dance around the lake with the mountains kissing the edges. It takes me back to the day I married Bertie on the edge of that same water. We didn't go for the typical ceremony. Hell no, we both tipped our toes in the water as we took our vows then jumped in hand in hand off the dock during our reception.

"Dammit, Sasha." I kick at the ball of fur that I'd love to piss on. She growls back at me, baring her teeth. I give in. "Come here, baby girl."

Yep, just like a pussy, I bend down and scoop the princess up in my hands. She continues to growl as I fix my tie until it lies flat on my chest. I'm minutes away from taking my last few steps down the aisle. I can't fucking wait to rush to my girls at the end of the aisle on the sandy beach. My beginning started and now has ended with her. I've felt guilt over my yesterdays, but not today. It's the moment of time where I'll start my forever.

"Dad!" Blonde wild curls peek into the room. "It's time."

Sasha claws at my collar, digging into my skin. The little shit leaps out of my arms, landing on all four paws.

"Let's get it done, baby girl."

And now our two girls play and splash out in the same water where all our lives we joined together as one. There was no looking back. Our future was too damn bright.

We bought up all the surrounding land, developing cabins. Yeah, that "we" includes Jessie and Max and their families. It's our little slice of heaven we get to escape to, and the older we grow, the more we find ourselves up here. Jules travels along, making it perfect for schooling the children.

We men rock on the porch, sipping on whiskey while studying our future. I'm still unable to comprehend how fast life can change. My bar is still thriving, but under the operation of my manager, Deacon. I continue watching our kids. Finn has grown real fond of Cody, and I have no damn delight in that fact. He may be Max's son, but that's my daughter.

"If his shoulder brushes my daughter's again, I'm gonna go dunk him, giving him a real life lesson," I growl.

Jessie chuckles. He's been through this whole game with Whit and Zack. But it's a whole new ball game when it comes to your own daughter.

Something has been up with Whit and Zack, but some topics are off limits when we're indulging on the porch. I could guess it's pretty damn typical in the fact Zack broke Whit's heart and now we all hate the slimeball.

Max puffs on his cigar. "They're walking. Chill the shit out."

I growl back at him.

When Cody sits on the sandy beach, Finn sits right next to her, wrapping his arm around her shoulder. Before I have the chance to lose my ever-loving shit, the women "ooh" and "ahh."

"They're so cute together. I called it the day they met," Jules sings out.

"They are perfect," Kate adds.

A warm petite hand settles on my shoulder, and a whisper tickles my ear. "It's okay, daddy grizzly bear. They are twelve."

"Bullshit," I grumble. "I'll break his fingers and don't give a shit whose son he is."

"Calm down, papa bear." Bertie leans down, placing a sweet, tender kiss on my cheek. "This is only the beginning."

I don't have a chance to respond or lose my shit because Robby decides to dive off the boat dock. I'm up and on my feet, pounding the short distance. I sprint down the sandy beach, panic gripping my chest. I'm a few feet away as she resurfaces, fist pumping the air. Her toothy grin is on display while her blonde curls are wet down to her cheeks. By damn, Bertie isn't only the love of my life, smart as shit, and caring as hell, but she reproduces little mini-me's. You'd have no idea Robby was mine. She is a mirror image of Bertie and my daughter, Cody.

"Dad." My other daughter is at my side. "I told her not to do that, but she never listens. I swear she's so dang stubborn."

I bite back the slice of laughter that threatens to escape at my girl's antics. She loves and hates her little sister as much as she did Scotty.

Cody follows me down the boat dock until I'm reaching my hand down, tugging Robby out of the water with no life jacket in sight. Nope, just some damn hot pink polka-dot bikini. If you all thought Cody loved yellow, then Robby was made of hot pink, glitter, piss, and vinegar. The damn girl will be the death of me. Her smile blinds me as she shimmies her hips.

"Robby," I growl, doing my best not to crack a smile.

"Daddy." She props her hands on her hips as her feet settle on the dock.

"Robby." I stare right back at her. "How many times have I told you about water and life jackets?"

"Yous told me when we were watching the Ompics at the bar that I could win a gold and I went for that." She bats her wet lashes at me. And I'm a damn goner.

The people who gave me life will never know the miracles that have followed. Every single day I wake up next to a doctor that saved my life and stole my heart followed by two brilliant blonde beauties who inevitably bound between us are the sweetest loves of my life. No amount of whiskey could or will replace that feeling. The day Robby explained to her mom what was in the Pussy Pleaser, my signature drink, at the bar, I did fear for my life. It only took a little loving and smooth talking before I had my doctor back in my good graces.

"For shit sakes." I drop to my knees.

Robby covers her mouth. "You said shit, Daddy, shit, shit, shit!"

For Christ sakes, I bite down on my bottom lip. "I did, and that's because you scared the shit out of me."

"Why, Daddy? You said I can be in the Ompics, and I just nailed that." She winks at me.

God bless this little girl who has the smarts of her momma and sister and my damn slick charm. The world has no idea what is coming their way. None.

"She has no hope." Cody shakes her head, going to take off.

I don't miss the chance to wrap her up in a hug and kiss the top of her head. She still loves yellow and Sasha, but not so much a Daddy's girl anymore. I'd never admit to anyone that it crushes my soul.

Cody goes back to Finn, sitting way too damn close for my comfort, and Robby takes another dive head first off the boat dock before I have the chance to grab her damn tiny swimming suit. I tear the shirt off my back, readying to dive in after her. When there are air bubbles, I collapse on my ass on the harsh dock, shaking my head. This little shit will be the death of me.

I never knew that three strong-willed women would be my undoing. But they are also my greatest saviors. I'll bask in their crazy, love, and sweetness every day of my life, never regretting a damn thing.

A splash near my toes catches my attention, and then a warm hand trails up my thigh. I glance over to the prettiest girl I ever did see. Blonde crazy curls are piled up on her head, and loving eyes shine back at me. My girl. My doctor. My love.

"She's all you, Cody Sterling." She winks at me. "I do believe it's called karma."

I nod and smirk then take privilege of gracing my lips against her sweet ones. "The best kind of karma."

She squints her eyes at me. "Tell me that in a few years, Cody Sterling."

I lean over and kiss the hell out of her, not giving her an answer. Because the truth is with her at my side, I'll never need any armor. My girl, the love of my life, wife, and mother of my children. Our story will never end. Yesterdays were my biggest regret and now my greatest salvation.

***

Did you enjoy YESTERDAY IS OURS? Check out more works by HJ Bellus on Amazon!

Acknowledgments

Wow, another one down and boy am I in love with Cody and Bertie's story. It was raw at times and beautiful in others. Thank you so much for taking time out to read my words. It means everything. You readers are truly the rock stars! I will forever be grateful you make this wild ride possible.

Love,
HJ Bellus

About the Author

HJ Bellus is a small-town girl who loves the art of storytelling. When not making readers laugh or cry, she's a part-time livestock wrangler that can be found in the middle of Idaho, shot gunning a beer while listening to some Miranda Lambert on her Beats and rocking out in her boots.

Join my newsletter:
http://bit.ly/2Lwofma

Facebook:
https://www.facebook.com/AuthorHjBellus

Twitter:
https://twitter.com/HJBellus

Goodreads:
https://www.goodreads.com/HJBellus

Join our Reader Group on Facebook and
don't miss out on meeting our authors and
entering epic giveaways!

Limitless Reading

Where reading a book
is your first step to becoming
limitless...

LIMITLESS PUBLISHING *Reader Group*

Join today! *"Where reading a book is your
first step to becoming limitless..."*

https://www.facebook.com/groups/Limitle
ssReading/